Ground Burst

Book 4 of the Sheriff Bullet Mysteries

Written by S. G. Lee

Acknowledgments:

Sincere thanks to Jodi and Sydney, without your
constant support and encouragement, this book would
not be possible. You are the best friends a writer
could have. I dedicate this book to my daughters, my
son-in law and my husband; who have supported my
writing endeavours with encouragement and love.
Special thanks to my beloved mother and sister in
heaven, who taught me dreams, can come true with
hard work, perseverance and patience.

Table of Contents

Preface ……………….....................1

Chapter 1 – Cruel
Perfection.....................................13

Chapter 2 – Crash Site................19

Chapter 3 –FEDS Stand for
Interference..................................25

Chapter 4 – Old Friends and Enemies, Make
Bad Business.................................29

Chapter 5 – Something is Rotten in the State
of Denmark…….............................48

Chapter 6 – Life's a Bitch and Then You
Don't Die...……….........................55

Chapter 7 – Rescue Me…….........61

Chapter 8 – My Least Favorite
Place..65

Chapter 9 – Back to Driftwood
…………..95

Chapter 10 – Uncle Tommy Never Learned to
Played Ball……………………….103

Chapter 11 –Prepare for Disaster, Recover
Faster…………………………….112

Chapter 12 -School Days Adult Play Days
……………………………………...122

Chapter 13 – Former cops don't play fair
………………….............................126

Chapter 14 – Who was Stella-Marie's
Savior…………………………………135

Chapter 15 – On the case……………157

Chapter 16 – The Worst Possible
Outcome……………………………….162

Chapter 17 – Confusion Reigns …….171

Chapter 18 – Election Woes…………179

Chapter 19 – Criminal Enterprise is moving
into Driftwood……………...................189

Excerpt from External Ballistics…....196

Excerpt- From Jack Be Nimble……...203

Excerpt from A Penny Saved A Murder
Earned………………….....................220

Excerpt from Love's Labour's Won...255

Excerpt From Stray Bullet…………...291

Excerpt from Dreams Can
Kill………………………………….329

List of Books by S.G. Lee……………357

Preface:

The weather in Driftwood, had gone from warm to cold, and light snow was falling. Despite it being August 20th, we were now getting a light dusting. Nothing new for Colorado, as in the mountains it could snow year-round. Stella-Marie would be flying home on Friday with Aunt Louise; I should have been happy; but it was calm, crime-wise and that worried me. Okay, so, I was covering Teardrop Canyon the next-door county; because the sheriff was out sick, and they had no one who could order the underlings, It was relatively easy as it was a sleepy little town, much smaller than Driftwood, with no crime.

Maybe, I was just an adrenaline junky, I thought; but still the lingering feelings remained of unease. Perhaps it was Uncle Tommy's present of a Faraday cage. For those of you who have never heard of this cage, mine was a small box like contraption with wire mesh and added metal plates, shielding the bugs from working in my office. Why did I need this? Uncle Tommy had swept my office and found recording devices. Did someone hope to get some dirt on me? Did they want to win the election that bad? It was silly, I had nothing to hide.

Uncle Tommy said he was on top of it, but I had told him to butt out. The Faraday cage was enough.

I'd helped Frankie Banks through the murder trial of his uncle and placed him in a good foster home. Frankie was blooming and probably would soon go to the college of his choice with his score on the 1600 SAT's, he scored. Many colleges would now be courting him. In fact, his ordeal with his uncle would play in his favor if he chose to tell the story they insisted. I told them I hoped it was his choice. They assured me it was. So that was my last worry, the kid would be okay despite being related to a dead drug lord, Luis Cervantes and another murderous uncle who was also with a notorious drug and criminal gang. That branch of the family was certainly colorful.

I should just relax. The song by M. C. Hammer went through my head 'U can't touch this,' and I reached over to my I-phone to play it.

A siren going off outside my window in the town square. jarring me. I was sure there was no tornado. I hadn't received any weather warnings and it was snowing a little harder; so, what was the siren for? I turned off my I-phone and was just about to dial my cell phone when my desk phone rang.

"Sheriff Bullet?"

"This is Sheriff Bullet."

"I'm sure you've heard the siren going off. There's been an incident outside of town. I followed protocol and had the sirens activated, "Andrew declared.

"What's happened Andrew?"

"A train has derailed near my ranch and it was carrying chemicals which are leaching into ground water and then air."

"Shit!! Do you and Penny have gas masks Andrew?"

"Yes, but the town is going to be overwhelmed soon. Everyone needs to stay indoors and not to let air into their homes. They need to seal them tight."

"Tell, Gee, I'm on it. I sent out an alert on their phones; but he'll have to check on those in towns who don't have phones. There is a list in my top desk drawer," Penny interrupted in the background.

"Tell Penny, I said thanks."

"Sorry, Gee. I shouldn't have interrupted, but I thought Andrew was only speaking to me. I've been busy with the new hires," Penny said coming into my office.

"Names please, I wasn't here when Andrew hired them."

"Alan Pick," Penny started, but I interrupted her.

"Woah and I thought my first name was bad;. his last name is worse."

"It's actually even crueler, but don't let on you know, his birth name is Richard Pick, he just uses Alan. You better not tell either, Andrew. You haven't all ready unintentionally told anyone his name, have you?"

"I won't." Andrew stated.

"Parents should have licences to name children." I commented, "What is the other new officer's name?"

"It's Pete Volk. He angelized his name when he immigrated here. The papers he showed me say his real name is Petrov Volkov. But don't worry he's been a citizen since age 2 so no ICE worries there."

"I hate that we have to worry so much about ICE since the Republicans got on that band wagon. There not even in power and they are ruining things if Trump wins…."

"He won't and you'll win too you'll see," Andrew comforted me.

"I can see why Volk changed his name that's a real mouthful, but since my grandfather changed his name when he came here who am I to judge," I commented.

"There' s actually one more hire, Karl Antonov, as well." Andrew interrupted.

"Okay so that's it?"

"Yes, now I'm staying on scene until the safety board and other government officials get here, Gee."

"Thank-you Andrew. I'll get some men and we'll go visit the people on Penny's list.

I hung up the phone and was surprised to hear it ring immediately.

"Did you forget something, Andrew?"

"Mr. Bullet?"

'This is Sheriff Bullet."

"Oh. I didn't realize… I mean the phone number said this was a work number. I should have known that you were a sheriff."

"Who is this?"

"Louise's next-door neighbour and friend in Detroit, Gwendolyn Ashford."

"I'm afraid I don't remember your name, Ms. Ashford. My aunt has so many friends wherever she goes. Now what can I help you with?"

"I don't know how to tell you this, Mr. Bullet. Louise… She'd been sick for awhile; she begged me to take in your little girl a week ago. Louise thought she'd be fine in a few days and then fly home to you. Don't you worry about your little girl, she's fine."

"I still don't understand; why didn't she call me? Tell Stella-Marie that I'll come immediately."

But really, I was thinking I was being pulled in two directions, could I really leave now? But I obviously had to if Aunt Louise was ill but how?

"Louise didn't want to worry you, dear. She told me not to call you. She even told the hospital, that she had no relatives."

"Why?"

"She was afraid they'd seize Stella-Marie."

"But that wouldn't happen."

"I didn't think so, either; but Louise made me promise to call you if things got worse, only they got really worse and the hospital didn't call until she died."

"Died? What are you saying?"

"Louise passed away this evening. I haven't told Stella-Marie about her great aunt's death either. I just couldn't, you know?"

Gwendolyn Ashford then began loudly sobbing and I had to comfort her. A half- an hour later she began talking again, "Your

Aunt Louise had cancer ,when she was younger and apparently it came back last year. She got through the treatment and was in remission; but the doctors say that she had a weakened immune system and her heart gave out."

"How is my daughter?"

"Like I said, Stella-Marie doesn't know yet about her auntie. She's going to be really upset; but I promise to watch her until you get here."

I didn't know how I was going to leave and help my daughter. I had to do my duty and bury Aunt Louise. I was heartbroken; how would Stella-Marie feel? I had to go there; but Driftwood also needed me. I couldn't leave in the middle of a crisis.

My other line rang.

"Ms. Ashford would you hold on the line for a moment. I promise I'll pay for this call."

"Of course, dear. I'm sure you have important things to do after all you are the sheriff. I'll call back."

"I assure you this conversation is the most important thing on my mind, Ms. Ashford. Please stay on the phone."

"Very, well."

I put her on hold and took the call.

"Gunner, it's me."

"Uncle Tommy, thank goodness; I really needed to talk to you."

"Is it this chemical spill? Do you need help?"

"No, it's not that. I'm sorry to tell you this, but Aunt Louise has died of. a heart attack."

"What? That's impossible."

"She was vulnerable, because of an illness she had last year."

"The cancer? But she beat that."

"Her system was weakened."

"It's not fair; she was far too young. Younger than me. You know she wanted to be cremated, correct?"

"No, I didn't; but that makes sense."

"Will you have a celebration of Louise's life.?"

"Yes, but now. I've had to enforce council's restrictions of 10 people indoors and 50 outdoors. Other jurisdictions have dropped their restrictions ,but not our town. How can we do this? Aunt Louise will have more than 50; maybe we could have a zoom funeral? I can't leave, though what can I do?"

"Stay, I'll go and ship back Louise's ashes, I'll pick up Stella-Marie and fly her home while Anne works at the hospital. Don't you worry."

"Thank-you, Uncle Tommy."

"I loved her you know. In another lifetime, maybe, Louise would have loved me back; but then I wouldn't have moved on and married your Aunt Anne and Anne is my life. I've never loved anyone as I love Anne, but you're my family, too. I'm always here for you, Gunner. Never ever forget that I'm here for you."

"Aunt Louise helped raised me and was a mother to me."

"I know sonny boy. You still have me and Aunt Anne. We have no underline conditions and we're triple vaxxed and scheduled for the fourth shot next week. I'll get my shot moved up if I can then hit the airport."

"I love you, Uncle Tommy."

"I may not say it often, but I love you too. Now call your brother. You could use some more family."

"I will reach out, after I get to the senior citizens and anyone else that needs to be informed about the spill. Besides Blaze is visiting family at the rez. I don't to interrupt his family time."

"Okay, have it your way; brood, grieve and then get in touch. You should call your friend, Gordon Chum."

"Gordon's back with the F. B. I. he decided they were his people after all but he's had to take a demotion."

"Those bastards! Do you want me to put in a good word for him or your Aunt Anne to put in a good word?

"Thanks Uncle Tommy, but Gordon wants to handle this on his own."

"Fine, but reach out if you need anything. I'll see you in a few days, and I'll take good care of the poppet. I'll call you from Detroit. Bye now."

"Bye Uncle Tommy and thank -you."

"Take care of yourself, I've lost too many people and I need my nephews."

I reached out to talk to Ms. Ashford wasn't there. I tried to look up the directory of Detroit when Penny rang through and said, "A Ms. Ashford again on line one Sheriff."

"We were disconnected."

"Yes, sorry, Ms. Ashford.

I then told Ms. Ashford that I would make all the arrangements to bring my aunt and daughter home and then said goodbye. She didn't need to know Uncle Tommy was coming until it was necessary.

I grabbed my kit and gas mask and went into the community to make sure my people were safe.

Chapter 1 - Cruel Perfection

Walking around the train wreck site,

I couldn't believe how a few derailed cars could produce so much damage. The fiery balls were still filling the air with chemicals, which were leaching into the stratosphere. What could have caused an accident like this? Human error, sabotage, or both? Luckily for me, I'd soon have some help to find out why…though in fact, it really wouldn't be up to me, because the National Transportation Safety Board would determine probable cause of the accident. They would investigate with my assistance, only as a courtesy, but also, they had to use me simply because it was my county.

Soon, I'd be overrun by agencies, because lord knows if the F. B. I. thought there was an angle for them, they'd be here too. I wished Gordon was here, but he was back working for the F. B. I. .

I knew they wouldn't send him. They considered Gordon too close to me and seem to be afraid. Afraid, he'd do what? Conspire with me?

In the meantime, before they all got here, I was going to investigate on my own and protect the citizens of Driftwood in my own way. The first thing I needed to do was investigate the braking capabilities of this train and how these cars derailed.

I didn't know a lot about trains, so, what I didn't know, I looked up quickly on my computer.

I wasn't totally ignorant, I knew about throttles that controlled the speed of the engine and its cars I'd read about that as a kid,

Huh, apparently, gears were almost obsolete, most trains now adays used electric traction which is much more flexible than gears. Diesel fuels the generators from the combustion engine and converts the energy using an alternator, which runs the traction motors.

A train kind of floats on those railway tracks. The standard train track comprises two parallel steel rails set in a fixed distance apart, which is called the gauge. The standard gauge is typically 4 feet, 8.5 inches.

Okay. So, I needed to check the tracks were standard and in good shape before the accident. I decided to go to the library for more information. Books were concrete after all, and I like being old school.

The library was busy, but I quickly found a number of books that could give me information that were up to date. Thank goodness I and a number of other citizens had lobbied for library funding when the city planners had calculated deep cuts. It meant higher taxes but people had stood up for the library. Lucky for me this train was an older model train and did not operate with another independent electric line along the tracks. This would entail more investigating about electrical stuff, I had no idea about. I think that would even require someone who was an electrical engineer, or something not just some books that I couldn't quite comprehend.

I read on, noting most trains in the U.S. run on diesel, simply because we'd been more resistant to an electrical train that was so popular in Europe.

Which was good to know; but it did mean this was going to become a little more complicated than my understanding? Perhaps it was good that the other agencies would be investigating? No! They'd be in my business... the business of Driftwood and I'd have to assert my authority, making more work than usual. As if I didn't have enough to do watching the nearby county, Teardrop County as well.

I still had to know a little bit though, and if I was going to answer any intelligent questions, or even ask any questions, I needed to know more about trains.

The steel wheels on trains have tiny contact points, about the size of a dime. This contact point keeps them on those metal rails, but doesn't give them a lot of traction.

Hmm... could it be a traction problem?

No, traction probably wasn't the problem, Trains had no problem going around corners because the 'flanges' also known as projecting steel rims, kept them on track.

Wow!

Sand was sprayed on the tracks from a special compartment to increase the traction of the drive wheels, an electronic traction system applied the sand when the wheels slipped or if the engineer made an emergency stop.

Was any of this working at the time of the accident?

I'd love to have an answer for all these questions from the engineer; but he was beyond responding; unless I consulted a psychic. The conductor who was with the engineer was in a coma and it was looking good for him either.

The problem as I saw it, was that the cars had derailed. Gee, you're a genius Bullet!! Haha.!

What the hell were they carrying which was exploding like rockets? The trains were also leaching chemicals into the environment, that were going to have long term consequences on my community. I was reminded of how people lost their lives in other places in the world during these kinds of derailments and I worried more about my people.

Had everyone been evacuated? This was overwhelming, but at least it was keeping my mind off Aunt Louise's death if only for few minutes. I couldn't dwell, or even think about my grief, as long as my community was in danger. I checked out the books and left the quiet of the library.

The streets were bare, everyone seemed to be listening to my orders to stay inside, but I needed to see the containment site for myself. I donned my protective gear and got in my jeep and headed to the crash site.

~0~

Chapter 2 – Crash Site

As I entered the zone, I passed the check points and acknowledged; that my men were keeping people out. Then I saw the woods beside the train derailment. Although some of the woods had gone up like tinder, the fire was contained and it had not spread further into the wooded area, which meant people could come through the woods and onto the crash site. I needed to post someone here.

Just as I thought that, I saw a woman exiting the woods and run to a nearby home. That home was on fire. I rushed to stop her. She shouldn't be in the zone let alone trying to enter a burning home.

It was then I recognized her, it was Tais Gilbert (a librarian from our local library, downtown) who I had met briefly, while researching some information needed for my job.

"Ms. Gilbert, Tais please stop; you can't go in there."

Tais kept on going towards the front door, as if she didn't hear me. I ran from my patrol car; but before I got there, Tais entered the burning home.

I ran in after her, grateful for my hazmat suit and MIRA Safety gas mask with a full-face respirator. Tais had on a face mask, but that was all. Tais really wasn't protected. What was so important ,Tais dashed back into her home? The smoke was thick, and I stumbled over some furniture, before I heard Tais coughing and followed the sound to her bending over a body.

"Help me; it's my son, Gino. He went back for his Gameboy."

I helped her carry Gino outside; he couldn't have weighed more than a hundred pounds, but he seemed much more than that as he was unconscious. I laid him down outside and summoned an ambulance.

Lucky for both of them, paramedics were actually standing around outside, they assessed Tais and Gino. Tais required some oxygen and so did Gino. Gino was breathing a little better and then took him and his mother to the hospital for further evaluation. I worried however, that it had been too easy for Gino to come home and enter the house. Even if it was safe for people to enter their homes (which it was not) looters could decide to enter the temporarily unoccupied homes. I quickly rallied some people (deputizing them) to guard the traffic from the forest area.

"Sheriff?" someone said on my right.

"Andrew?"

"I think I've found what derailed the train."

"Spit it out then!"

"It was a sinkhole, sir."

"A sinkhole? I thought they were only in Florida. Where did you find a sinkhole?"

"Under the tracks, where the train flipped over,(just behind the rise), I first found tree roots exposed and then a sinkhole directly under the train tracks," Andrew stated, pointing,

"I understand the basic information of sinkholes, I think. The ground collapses and the soil, or dirt moves downward creating a sinkhole, but I thought the soil was too dry right now to do this." I said, quickly googling the information on my phone.

"We've had a lot of snows and rains, this year, followed by long periods of drought and then more rain. These are ripe conditions for sinkholes," Andrew said confidently.

"But aren't sinkholes created by areas with certain types of minerals in their soil?" I asked.

"I'm not sure, but we must have some of those minerals in our soil, because we do have a sinkhole that could have possibly caused this train derailment."

"Then we must have some kind of limestone, dolomite, and gypsum in table called Karst terrain according to the internet article, I'm reading."

"That can't be good."

"No, it can't be good. According to this article, however, they can happen anywhere on the terrain if we have any of those minerals."

Someone else started yelling and I heard them say that some cars had travelled further down the line and were now derailed some twenty, or thirty miles down the track. The problem with that is the area wasn't easily accessible. How could a sinkhole have created all this?

"Shit! Boss I think this is getting worse."

"The thing I'm worried about is if we have more sinkholes down the line then are there any others in other parts of the county we should be worried about. There is a lot of territory to cover. Should we be worried above evacuating even more citizens, Andrew?"

"We 're stretched to the limit now, boss, in man power. Those cutbacks city council made us do are hurting us; how are we going to checkout this new site; let alone the county?"

"I have some ideas that might help," I commented.

I then made a rapid call to my Uncle Tommy who was in the air on the way to Detroit. Luckily for me, his phone was turned on and he quickly agreed to loan me his helicopter in the hangar on his property.

He advised me where to find the key and told me, not to forget to file a flight plan. As if I was a first-year pilot!! Then I realized Uncle Tommy had two reasons, distraction and because he was genuinely worried about me.

"I'm hanging in there, Uncle Tommy. Just get my little girl home, while I take care of business here."

"Love you, sonny boy. Take care of yourself, and my helicopter, see you soon," Uncle Tommy replied.

~0~

Chapter 3 – FEDS Stand for Interference

I drove to my office, chucking my coat off. I'd have to take the coat to the dry cleaners soon; it smelled of chemicals. I entered the outer area of the Sherriff's office. Andrew called me on my cell phone. I thought that odd wasn't he in the building?

"Boss, I have to talk to you more about this derailment."

"The F. B, I, and The National Transportation Safety Board will be here soon, Should I wait for them, or take the bird up and get a look at this train peril further up the line, Andrew?"

"Boss, I was also supposed to tell you there are F. B. I. agents in your office," Andrew answered.

"Not in my actual office," I protested.

"No, I wouldn't violate your privacy, I put them in the outer office. Your office is locked. I'd never let anyone in your inner sanctum."

"How many agents are there besides, Gordon?" I asked hopefully.

"Mr. Chum isn't there. sir."

"Damn, who did they send?"

"Two women, I'm sorry, I don't remember their names, also your brother was here."

"Blaze is back and talking to agents? Wow that would be a change."

"He hasn't not seen them, sir. He saw you weren't here and said he'd be back."

"So, who is in my office?"

"Two women and a man who all say they are from the F. B. I."

"I'm almost at the office now. I'll talk to you, before I take my uncle's bird up to check out the other derailment down the line. I'd take you with me, but the truth is I need all the boots, I can get on the ground, I might need you to go over to Teardrop County for a few hours and check out their problems, until I can liaison better with them"

"I understand. We're about to take a step back now, I suppose."

"Not if I can help it, Andrew. Legally it's our county, they have to keep us in the loop."

"Good luck, boss, this is a tough bunch. They tried to make me give them details, but I held fast just like you taught and pretended like I knew nothing. Now, I know you, boss, you'll make them follow the letter of the law, so we keep jurisdiction."

"You bet your ass, I will. This is Driftwood and I'm dully elected law here not them."

"Practicing already boss?"

"I was that obvious?"

"Oh good, I see you walking in the station. I didn't hear, or see a thing. Never even saw you walk in either," Andrew chuckled.

"Wish me luck!" Now head over to
Teardrop County, I'll relieve you as soon as
I can," I said heading for my office and
hanging up my cell phone.

~0~

Chapter 4 - Old Enemies and Friends, Make Bad Business

In my office were two women, and a man.

The taller woman who stood about five eight, had red hair, and jade black eyes that twinkled like gemstones. Stunningly beautiful, she would have been the only focus of all the attention in the room, if it wasn't for the other woman, who was also stunning in her own right, The other woman was slightly shorter at five foot six, she had white blonde hair, pale blue eyes, encased in a pretty pair of glasses that seem to shade the light and very pale skin. The women even though they were stark opposites, looked alike to me. I guessed they were probably sisters, as I saw some kind of familial resemblance to each other.

"Sheriff Bullet? We are from the F. B. I ; I'm Agent Dai Summer and this is this is Agent Paul Jones and our tactician, Agent Stone Summer."

"I was expecting someone from the National Transportation Safety Board, not someone from the F. B.I., or should I say three people"

"Don't be glib," Jones sniped at me.

"Just who did you say you were, Agent?" I asked angrily, pretending I didn't know this little worm's name.

"According to one of our sources; (as we believe) this was an act of terrorism, so, Sheriff Bullet, we will be taking over this investigation. Although we may also have someone from the NTSA show up as well. "Jones continued.

"Doesn't matter while the National Transportation Safety Board has say over this kind of incidents and you and other agencies might want to step in; all of you have to realize that I have the final say in my county and I am the duly elected law in this county, not any of you."

"We understand that Sheriff Bullet, and we don't want to step on any toes." Agent Dai Summer interjected.

"Then don't!!"I quipped.

"Sheriff Bullet , let's not get into a pissing contest here, we all just want your cooperation to get to the bottom of this. Or we can go over your head…"Jones snarled.

"Jones…Don't be so confrontational. We can cooperate with Sheriff Bullet ;it is his county, "Agent Dai Summer insisted.

"No!" Jones blurted.

"I outrank you and as your superior officer, I order you to apologize to Sheriff Bullet and then…"

Just then my door flew opened and Blaze wandered in dressed in his cop uniform.

"Gee, I'm back and ready to help."

Then noticing the three bodies sitting in chairs he said, "Sheriff Bullet, I'm sorry I'm interrupting…what a minute Dai and Stoney? What are you doing here?"

"Blaze?" The two women blurted simultaneously.

"You know this cop, Dai and Stone?" Jones barked grabbing his pistol at his hip.

"Not that it's really any of your business, Jones, but we grew up with Blaze, and while are working in a professional capacity you will address us formally as I am your boss. Is that clear?" Agent Dai Summer spit out.

"We outrank you, you little worm…"Agent Stone Summer said clearly under her breath.

I hid a laugh, because she thought Jones a worm exactly, like I did. Then I realized Jones was insulting my brother with his behaviour. He might get away with some abuse of me, but he crossed the line with Blaze.

I glared at Jones, as his ferret-like eyes starring at Blaze with distrust and dislike.

"Back off Jones, you're a little snap happy. Number one this is my officer, not yours, number two, as Agent Dai Summer just told you, clearly it is really none of your business, what or who, comes into my office. If you wish to behave like a neanderthal. you can not only leave my office, but my county, too."

"Now gentleman. let's not get hasty," Stone commented.

Jones quit glaring, but I watched him warily.

"Arson, or vandalism, could be possibilities in the train derailment," Stone stated, trying hard to defuse the moment and get us back on task, "Other then terrorism. There are also potential ignition sources involving the train itself which we should look into.

"Equipment can be faulty, and you can get sparks," Jones interjected. "Bits of hot metal can also start fires. . . . Wheels of trains get hot. Sparks also can fly out of the train's exhaust system; that is if the system is not well maintained."

"We aren't neanderthals, we aren't a rinky-dink little county, you can overrun. We're not hicks and totally stupid. We have investigated the incident and are still investigating, but we've ruled out all the things you've just mentioned Jones." I interjected angrily.

"I think you should go to the hotel room and take our bags, Jones. We'll meet you there," Agent Dai Summer ordered.

Jones looked like he would balk, but he did as he was ordered.

Sheriff Bullet shall we go to the crash site?" Agent Dai Summer asked.

"Of course, you can, Agents Summer. Would you like to come along, Blaze?" I said in my most charming voice.

"I will remain behind. I am a tactician and legally blind and my guide dog, Oskâpêwis, aka Oskâ is at the vet," Agent Stone Summer replied.

"Great name for your dog, Stoney." Blaze commented.

"My dog's name means helper in Cree, even though I'm not Cree, as you well know."

"The vet who is looking after your dog, Oskâ has excellent references. She'll take good care of your dog and get him back to you very soon," Dai reassured.

"If I didn't have to work, I'd be there now," Stone commented.

"Oskâ will be back before we know it,' but we need your expertise on the case, Dai insisted.

"The smoke from your site is in the sir and when we arrived, Gadilid breathed it in and acted strange ,so as a precaution I took him into the vet next door," explained Stone.

"Doctor Barnes is a great vet. She's looked after my daughter's hamster," I admitted.

"That's a ringing endorsement. I'm so sorry about your daughter," Agent Stone Summer stated.

"My daughter is fine. I hid her, and my aunt so, that asshole, Luis Cervantes, couldn't find them. Now that he is dead, they could come home, except now my aunt can't …,I'm sorry Blaze. Aunt Louise died this morning," I said my voice breaking.

"Shit! What can I do? Gee, my god, what are you doing here, bro? I can take over go take care of the arrangements," Blaze insisted, "We can handle this."

"I am so sorry, Sheriff Bullet. You have our condolences. If you need to step away, we can take over.," Agent Dai Summer commented.

"Agent Summer good try, but I'm not leaving. I have this well in hand, my aunt and uncle will handle the details and bring the ashes back here. They also bring back my daughter to me, safe and well."

"You must like it a little too, informal in your office, Sheriff Bullet as you allow your subordinates to call you bro," Agent Stone Summer commented.

Blaze laughed a deep chuckle ,which came from a well deep inside him. he was laughing so loud. I felt he'd fall on the floor. I couldn't help it; I started laughing too.

"What is so funny?' Agent Dai Summer asked.

"Blaze is my half- brother," I explained.

"What, but I thought you were an only child, Blaze?" Agent Dai Summer blurted.

"We only found out a short time ago, that we have the same mother, but we've bonded like we grew up together. Must have been from almost dying, defeating that bastard Luis Cervantes," Blaze explained.

"Wow," Agent Stone Summer said.

Something passed between them, almost like I could see a spark. Blaze was definitely attracted to Stone Summer. Had they had something before? I looked again, oh yes, most definitely they had clicked in the past in some form.

"Agent Dai Summer and I will take my uncle's bird up. We would like to access the area and make sure we have no more problems, or sinkholes"

"Sinkholes? They are sinkholes? Could that have caused all of this disaster?" Stone asked.

"Yes, you could be correct, Agent Summer, but it was more I think," Dai commented.

"You think it might be sabotage, or terrorism combined?" Blaze asked.

"I would like to get a bird's eye view of the area and of course wait for the experts' analyzation of the chemical composition of the results the train wreck."

"What a bunch of gobble-gook, Dai. If you need to show us that you are tough you can; but my brother and I, are both down to earth you don't have to do technical speech with us to sound like you know how to do the job."

"Shut-up Blaze," Stone said in a warning tone

"Deputy Trail, I appreciate your input, but this is a conversation between your sheriff and I."

"Well la-di-da!!"Blaze spouted.

"Sorry, Sheriff Bullet. I'll get right on that," Blaze answered using a hurt tone, but took out the sting with a wink in my direction that neither woman could see.

Blaze soon left directing Agent Summer.

"Sorry about that."

"It's hard to work with family," complained Agent Dai Summer.

My phone rang it was Uncle Tommy, again; but I ignored it silencing it.

"Blaze is okay, but I do have to enforce work decorum. I have a reputation to uphold and with friendships and family they tend to cross the line, repeatedly."

"I know the feeling. Now tell me, how are we going to get a bird's eye view is there a lookout tower, or does your department miraculously have a helicopter in this small town? "

"No, but my uncle has generously offered me his personal helicopter. It's in a hanger at the airport."

"That is convenient. When can we go? "

"Now!"

Agent Summer followed me to my car, as we drove to the hanger my phone buzzed again. I thought, I'll get back to Uncle Tommy, after our excursion. Once there the security guard recognized me told me that Uncle Tommy had called and I was good to go, but that we'd better get going because the forecast was for some fog to roll in.

"Great! It will carry those fumes further through the county," I complained.

"Wow, a two-seater, ultra-light? Those costs some big bucks. Is there something I should know about your uncle?"

"My uncle was a CEO of a huge company, before his retirement and has lots of investments. This helicopter is merely one of his retirement toys, given to him by one of his friends."

"Is that the story he's going with? While, okay, as long as they're not illegal funds, I have to report."

I gave her an incredulous look and she winked at me. There was a lot more to this woman then I knew. I would have to keep on my toes.

We got in the chopper and I loaded my equipment. I also packed two parachutes. Agent Dai Summer noticed and said, "Are you that bad a helicopter pilot? I have a licence I can fly, too, I'll have you know."

"I just believe in being prepared."

"You know, sometimes a parachute won't help you."

"Yes, but I'm betting it will."

"Let's get this show on the road," Dai Summer insisted.

"Call me Gee, when we're alone."

"Sure, if you call me Dai."

We'd just stepped into the ultra-light helicopter when my phone rang again.

" I have to take this call it's my Uncle Tommy and he won't quit ringing my phone, so it's urgent."

"Please go ahead but make it quick you heard the man., fog is rolling in later and I'd like to be back on land before that.

I stepped out of the helicopter and took the call.

"Now is not a good time, Uncle Tommy. What's up?"

"My rental car blew up, that's what up"

"What? Are you and Aunt Anne, okay?"

"Anne is working at the hospital with the derailment, she felt she couldn't possibly leave."

"So, you're all alone. You are obviously okay, or you would have said something, wouldn't you have?"

"I'm fine, no thanks to whoever put the hit out. I've hired some muscle to protecting me now, and I'm not taking any unnecessary chances."

"A hit, you think that it was a hit? You are just telling me this all now? Why a hit? Do you think they knew it was you, Uncle Tommy, arriving in Detroit? But how?"

"If I hadn't stopped for breakfast at the diner and parked in the back parking lot..."

"Good grief, was anyone hurt?"

"No, thank God; but I had to call Anne to talk to the investigating officer The man was single-minded and pointing in my direction, like I had something to do with all this."

"Did you?"

"Not you too, sonny boy."

"All I meant was is someone is after you. How did they know you were in Detroit?"

"The rental car was in the name Bullet, son. That means that it could have been meant for you, too. So, I put out some feelers and then I called the funeral home to tell them I was delayed and..."

"And what? Spit it out."

"The number that Mrs. Ashford gave us doesn't exist, but then neither does she."

"What? But if she doesn't exist then what's going on? Where's Aunt Louise's body. Is Stella-Marie, okay?"

"I haven't been able to find out yet, sonny, but I will. Now it also means that we don't really know that your Aunt Louise is dead."

"Aunt Louise is alive?"

"Don't get your hopes up! Someone may have perpetrated a hoax on us son, but specifically it may have been a hoax to lure you. First, they told you, your aunt was dead and then the car is blown up; you have to realize that all of this is very suspicious!"

"You have to find out where my daughter is and if my aunt is alive."

"I'm getting another call. This might be some information I was waiting on; I'm going to put you on hold, stay on the line. I promise to be quick," Uncle Tommy insisted.

I couldn't believe it .What the hell was going on? Was someone after me personally, or was it an attack on Uncle Tommy? Uncle Tommy had a lot of enemies and if one of them found him...

"Are you sitting down ,boyo? Your Aunt
Louise took a trip to Stepping Stone Falls
and they were on a river cruise, when my
people found them. Your Aunt Louise just
wanted to give Stella-Marie some fun;
before they left for Driftwood on Friday.
She' s probably going to be calling you from
a landline, soon because she lost her cell
phone. Personally, I think someone nicked it
from her, so I put some guards on her.
Whoever perpetrated this hoax won't be able
to get to Stella-Marie, or Louise."

"Isn't it to soon for you to know that it
wasn't an accident, that the gas tank just
exploded?

"If it looks like a duck, swims like a duck,
and quacks like a duck, then it probably is a
duck."

"But who is behind all this Uncle Tommy?"

"I don't know ,but we're going to find out. I
told you I have lots of feelers out, ,and a guy
overseeing the work at the cop shop to make
sure it's done faster."

"You trust these guys? They can keep Aunt
Louise and Stella-Marie safe?"

"They would lay down their lives to protect them. They can stay with them in in Driftwood."

"I don't think the place ,I bought in Driftwood is safe for my aunt and my little girl even with guards,"

"You should all move in with me ,until it is resolved. I have armed guards patrolling, electrified fencing and arms up the ying yang on the house. There is also a fortified safe room that can with stand mortar rounds, plus an extra cottage in case we need more help."

I laughed because it was either that or cry, here we were again, under siege; but by whom? One of Uncle Tommy's mobster enemies, or one of my enemies. Don't get me wrong, I was extatically happy that Aunt Louise wasn't dead, that her demise had been a hoax; but someone had bombed the car. We were all in danger, until Uncle Tommy and I found out who had perpetrated the bombing and the death hoax.

"I'll take you up on your offer, but only because of Aunt Louise, Stella-Marie and Blaze."

"I'll take it boyo, stay safe."

"I will. I'm about to take your chopper up
we'll talk soon."

"I'll tell your Aunt Louise, that she can
reach you in a couple of hours."

"Bye for now, stay safe yourself."

I wanted to look into this some more and
stay on top of it, but I had to trust that Uncle
Tommy was doing just that. Right now,
however, I had to fly this chopper and show
Agent Dai Summer the crash site, the
sinkholes and other areas that might be
affect by ground changes. I had a job to do
here ;as my father's brothers would have
told me 'I best get to it.'"

"I heard some of that, should we go back to
the hanger and do this another time?" Agent
Summer asked.

"I want to do my job, the job I stayed here in
Driftwood for, while Uncle Tommy went to
retrieve my aunt's remains.

"It sounds like someone is trying to gaslight
you and lure you to that city so they can kill
you. Do you have any enemies?"

 "As a cop there's always enemies, you
know that better than most, Agent Summer.

I need to look after my people and my uncle can handle this along with my aunt's contacts."

"If you say so."

"I do say so, let's head over the crash site and I'd also like to get a look at adjacent where my deputy says sinkholes are forming."

"Lead on Sheriff Bullet."

"I'm no Macbeth, lucky for you."

Dai Summer chuckled ,and I thought she smiled; but I couldn't be sure. Maybe we could be friends after all?

~0~

.

Chapter 5 – Something is Rotten in the State of Denmark

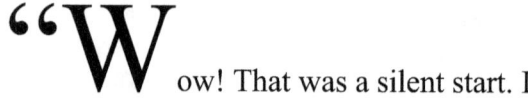"**W**ow! That was a silent start. I
haven't been up in a model like this before,
but it certainly is smooth, "Agent Dai
Summer commented.

As I cruised at 150 km. the first indication I
had that something was wrong with the two-
seater, was the shaking in the clutch system.
It wasn't like I had reached the maximum
speed of 194km, in fact I'd planned on the
higher speed just for a couple of minutes,
until we got over the site.

I adjusted my grip and took the bird a little
higher, thinking that would fix the problem.
After all I had done my simulator training on
this model with Uncle Tommy, or he
wouldn't have let me borrow his new toy. It

didn't make any difference, and that's when I heard the rotator blade on the tail, make an odd noise screeching noise. Warning lights were blinking at me, until they suddenly stopped, like someone had thrown a switch.

"What's wrong?"

"Not sure, but the rotator (as you can hear) is making odd sounds and now the dashboard lights have given out. Maybe I better get on the horn, and tell them we're making an emergency landing."

"I'm on it," Dai flipped a switch and began talking into the microphone, but we were dead on all channels.

I took out my cell and found something odd, it was like something electronic had switched everything off. Dai took out her cell phone and found the same thing. Something was jamming them. Someone was jamming us!

"I'm going to find an open field and land this bird."

Agent Summer got up and walked to the back of the helicopter.

I thought she was walking out of stress; much to my surprise in the next minute Agent Dai Summer's black moonstone, shaped eyes ,grew wide ,and she looked terrified.

"I'm going to put on that extra parachute you brought, maybe you should do the same." she stated calmly.

"We aren't that desperate. I can land us safely and protect any structures, or people below, while I'm at it."

"I don't think so," Agent Summer said, handing me a parachute.

Frankly, I was insulted, she thought I was incapable?

"Don't look at me that way! You can't get up right now to see this, but there's a bomb on the tail rotator"

"Are you sure?"

"What kind of stupid question is that? We need to jump of this tin can."

"Don't panic Agent Summer, but we have a slight problem."

"If we're going to die, shouldn't we call each other by our first names? My name is Dai okay Daiyiilah (I pronounce it like Deilah) Aiukli 'pronounced eye-yuke-lee', Summer but if you tell anyone...."

"My name is mud?"

"That's about it."

"I'm Gee."

"What's the G. stand for; it's like someone scraped the internet and all the records. I couldn't find a thing and I tried."

"It's Gunner, but if you tell anyone…"

"You'll have to scrub me?" Dai said laughing.

I smiled.

"What the hell are we doing? We need to get out of this death box!" Dai exclaimed.

"You need to go first. I've done this before, and you only have 10 or more seconds to fall clear of rotor-wash before opening the parachute and if the rotator explodes and falls off, the craft will fall straight down out of the sky."

"That's all?"

"Yes, there must be a timer; what if we don't have any time?"

"We will just have to assume we do. You have the parachute on, time to make that jump. Remember, count less than 10 seconds to get clear."

"Will do, then you'll jump?"

"First, I have to make sure this chopper won't take out buildings, or someone on the ground."

"But you have to jump."

'I will know get going."

Dai reluctantly jump and I watched as she made the jump cautiously, and accurately within the time window. She waved to from the ground gathering up the parachute.

I steered the helicopter towards where I knew there was an open field. That's when I found a bomb, hidden under the dashboard. So, that's why the lights were out, as well as communication. Just my luck two bombs someone wanted me dead, or perhaps Uncle Tommy.

Shit! I had six minutes according to the timer for that one. Could they be timed to go off together, or was the tail rotator bomb going to go off first?

The chopper violently yawed in the opposite direction of the main rotor's rotation. Then the helicopter began to pitch even more radically, nose-down.

I realized with growing apprehension any marginal assistance, an intact tail boom, and vertical tail might give with directional control while the aircraft continued to move forward, would be largely negated, not only because of the loss of the tail rotator, but because the navigational control had ceased to work. I had to get out of here fast, and time it so I didn't get sucked up in the updraft of the falling helicopter.

I had seconds, for once the tail rotator came
off it would seesaw and once the tail boom,
was gone it would plumet straight down,
possibly upside down to my death. The tail
rotator bomb exploded right at the moment,
I jumped, or so, it seemed.

I said my prayers and plummeted
downward.

~0~

Chapter 6 - Life's a Bitch and Then You Don't Die

I woke up in a tree, hanging upside down, about ten feet off the ground. In the distance I saw the chopper, smoke filling the air and sparks climbing up almost to the sky, flames flickering, teasing that they could jump to fan, some glowing trees. I couldn't tell whether the helicopter was still in one piece, but even upside down, I doubted it. There was no clearing in any direction, only trees. Hopefully the trees weren't all like tinder and I hadn't started a forest fire that would kill me first.

I took stock of my body and found my left ankle had taken a beating; it might even be broken. The rest of my body, I thought was probably okay, but it felt bruised, like I had hit every tree branch, before ending up here.

Dia had landed safely, but that was some miles from me and with the dead zone we were in, my cell phone didn't work, did hers? Hopefully, she'd find her way to civilization and be safe; but we were way off course.

I hadn't told her that the helicopter had accelerated to full throttle and therefore, when she had jumped, she was close to, or in the Gunnison National Forest .Even further in the forest from me (given the distance that must have occurred before I jumped when the helicopter crashed.) All of this meant rescue would be more difficult, especially, because there had been no mayday.

Sounded like something straight out of a hero movie or television show; but the truth is I was no hero, I got lucky and had survived this attempt to kill me, or Uncle Tommy. I was scared. I was in the middle of nowhere and this forest had recently had a spate of what could only be termed as mysterious deaths, possibly from a serial killer. Did I have my gun still?

Yes, it was secure in my holster with the safety on and I had a backpack with food and water and bullets on my front. I shouldn't panic, I was the sheriff; get your head in the game, Bullet!! I ordered myself.

I examined my head and found a goose egg on the back of my head and small amount of blood. Great, a head injury. Probably wasn't too serious, right? No wooziness, that was a plus, and I was thinking clearly (except for the self-doubting). I only had a small headache so, no problem.

Hopefully, Dia was on the outskirts of the edge of the Gunnison National Forest. Dia would be safe; I told myself and she could get to help quicker who would then come looking for me... maybe. If they even had a clue where I was.

As for me, I had to fend for myself, get down from this fuckin' tree and get to civilization. Someone had tried again to kill ether, Uncle Tommy, or me .

I had to discover who they were trying to kill and who was behind this, before they succeeded in killing one, or both of us, or someone close to us by accident. . I had a plan now, that was clear thinking. See no head injury which would stop me. Ankle injury? No problem, I was a Bullet we were invincible, at least that's what my uncles always told me.

I bent my body up, until I could reach my pocket knife in my pants pocket. Flipping the knife open, I cut the strands of the parachute wrapping it around the tree scaling down the tree with the pieces of parachute. Anchored with the parachute belt, Wrapping the rope around the tree, I shimmied down the tree. Every push with my left foot nearly killed me, as I wanted to scream out in pain, but I grinned and bore it. I had to get to the ground.

A few minutes later, I found myself on the ground removing the remains of the parachute and laughing with glee, when I found the pieces, I had cut from it above nearby. I took some pieces of parachute and wrapped my ankle.

It helped a little, but it was swelling up and I knew I would be walking nowhere without an aid. I grabbed a tree branch and with my trusty Swiss army knife managed to fashion a crutch.

The rest of the parachute I rolled up ,it would make a tent in a pinch;(and I might need one; depending on how long it took me to reach civilization, or a searcher found me) especially with the ropes which I had transformed for my trip, down the tree.

I began walking still seeing my helicopter smouldering I the distance. Then it began to rain, not just a light rain but an epic downpour. Streams of torrential rain coming down so fast I started to worry about flash floods again. I mean hadn't I survived that already? The only good part of it was I was now going upward in elevation I saw the flames go out from the crash. I was drenched to the bone I needed to get war or I risked hypothermia. Yes, even in late August.

I saw a cave like structure and with trepidation ,I decided to risk going in there; hoping a bear hadn't made its home there.

I took the lighter out of my backpack, some twigs and lit a small fire. Pouring some water into the metal cup from my backpack, I heated some water and stuck in a teabag from my meager food supply. I then saved the teabag in some plastic lacing. in the backpack for future use.

I took off my coat and let it dry near the fire, while the clothes, I was wearing also

warmed and dried. I was tired, but I was also
leery of predators ,coming upon me sleeping
so, I fell into a light sleep using the
parachute as a down cloth, and a blanket as
well.

~0~

Chapter 7 - Rescue Me

As I walked into the beginnings of the old town, I saw a decrepit cabin, brown and weathered with wooden slats, which had seen better days in Crystal, Colorado. This was after all, a virtual ghost town in the valley, on the upper Crystal River, in Gunnison County. There were no people here, only snow and a road rutted with four-wheel-drive divots, but I had to maneuver it as it was the only road between here and Marble.

I better pick up the pace, I thought then I looked at my left ankle, it was swelling up so much. I'd have to bandage up it and carry my boot, or it would have to be cut off to save my ankle.

I tied my boot to the backpack with the laces
and then wrapped my ankle some more to
keep it warm; but oddly enough the cold air
actually felt good on the left ankle. Was that
good, or bad?

I hobbled down the road and thought I was
doing very well, until I hit a hidden rut,
covered in snow, which knocked me on my
ass.

I was almost ready to call it a day, when I
heard a rough, mechanical growl and then
the roars of more then one ATV machine,
headed my way. I tried to get up, but in the
mud and snow, I slipped again.

A burly muscled man dressed in a red jacket
and another smaller person on the other
ATV, dismounted and walked over to me.

The first man said, "Aren't you a sorry
sight! Maybe, next time, you'll learn to stay
with the crash vehicle in the event of a
crash!!"

"Chet, that's not fair! I think he's hurt."

"You found my bird? Is Dai, okay?" I commented, thinking this guy was a little too cocky (as my rescuer) for my tastes.

"No, we didn't find the helicopter, that's why we are so happy, that we found you," said the smaller person who from their voice and size, I thought was probably a woman.

"You didn't find my chopper? It is very hard to find it's on the edge of the Gunnison Forest. I can't tell you how far back, I just know that it was along journey to get here."

"We've been searching for four days, since you crashed and Agent Summer contacted us and a number of other volunteers to look for you."

"Four days? But it's only been two and half at best what day is it? I'm so glad Agent Dai Summer landed safely."

"It's August 24th. I'm Dale Linden and this Chet my brother. We'd like to get you to some medical help. Is it okay if my nitwit brother lifts you onto the back of my ATV?"

The other person was a guy? I was glad I hadn't said anything . I needed some more sensitivity training, obviously.

"Thanks for the rescue, Lindens; but no offence, I think the chopper crash was sabotage. Can I see some identification?"

"That F. B. I. woman said you'd insist on. You owe me 20 bucks Chet. Sheriff Bullet, I'd offer to let you use my cell, but this here town can be a real dead zone for cells.in fact I haven't been able to make a call all day. Chet got a signal though," Dale said, showing me her driver's licence and her local gun club membership. Chet then showed me his gun licence.

I had to take it on account that they were legitimate. I knew my ankle was done for; I couldn't travel any further on foot on it.

Chet and Dale were as good as their words and they soon had driven me to the Health Care Center in town but I couldn't say it wasn't a bumping ride and my head and ankle took the brunt of it.

~0~

Chapter 8 – My Least Favorite Place

After Dale explained that I had crashed four days ago ,a doctor at the Health Care Center took me ahead of the other patients, waiting in the emergency, Dale then left.

"You're a lucky man Mr. Bullet, your coverage seems to be adequate and will cover most tests you'll need; also, Marble is very lucky place to get sick in , there are 131 physicians per 100,000 population; so, you are in very good hands." said the nurse helping into a gown and up onto a stretcher.

Despite the nurse's statement, I wasn't reassured, I didn't want to be here; I needed to get back to Driftwood and my investigations.

"You need an Xray and a CT scan," the doctor said (as if I wasn't really there and

just an object) as he barked orders to the
nurse and then he left the room.

"When can I leave doctor? I need to call my
deputy to see what's going on in my town"

"Leave? Sheriff Bullet you were in
helicopter crash and you've asked me that
question three times, in the last fifteen
minutes. You've also already talked to your
deputy and your brother. I quote, you told
your brother to stay in Driftwood and listen
to everything Andrew said as he is in
charge, as acting sheriff. Now as for you,
you probably have a broken ankle which
might need surgery. You also have a head
injury. You need to stay here at the hospital
for a short time, so ,we can make sure
there's no lasting damage. Now just relax,
let me do my job and you can then do yours,
Sheriff!!"

The nurse injected something into my veins
and I passed out. I woke up with a cotton
mouth and Dai Summer sitting in a chair
next to my bed.

"Feeling better?"

"I feel like *Basil Fawlty*."

"I don't understand."

"*Fawlty Towers*."

"It's a British show from the 1970's. John Cleese is in it, and Connie Booth. My Aunt Louise and I used to watch it on DVD, when I was younger. She has the boxed set. The character **Basil Fawlty** had a head injury and he just agreed to everything his wife and the doctor said and then escaped from the hospital. When are we escaping?"

"Sorry, I can't possibly spring you, until at least tomorrow, against doctor's advice. You just had a surgery on your ankle and up until now ,you weren't making a lot of sense while I was here. You'll be hobbling on your ankle for a few weeks, while it heals, the doctor has said."

"Hey, your arm is in a sling and you're not sitting in a chair, you're also in a wheelchair," I stated noticing for the first time.

"Right again captain, obvious."

"You landed fine, when you jumped, didn't you?"

"Actually, I hit a tree on the way down, but unlike you I didn't hit the treetop and land upside down."

"You try jumping out of a crashing, bomb riddled helicopter!"

"I think I did; but thanks for giving me the extra time," Dai stated," I'd like to leave, but The F. B. I says I have to stay here and protect you until you leave."

"We could both hobble out of here, but you're going to observe me for twenty-four hours to make sure I can behave myself?" I asked wolfishly.

"I'm going to put that wild flirting down to your head injury and the fact that you can't seem to retain information more than a few minutes."

"You could do that, but I admit I'm a hopeless flirt with women. I'm attracted to, much like the man I look like. you know the movie/ television star I resemble. Except when I'm working of course no sexual harassment on the job."

"Then we'd better get you back to work. I understand that you and your uncle, are both under the impression ,you look like a poor man's Tom Selleck; nice try, cowboy! You are muscular, I freely admit (it's a must in our job) and you have a mustache, but you have more of younger Brendan Frasier look about you, where as, the picture I saw of your uncle looks like a cuddly, much older version of Brendan," Dia commented.

"Well thank you, ma'am."

"Don't let it go to your head, neither actor is my type. Now that we have that out of the way; we have to find out who sabotaged the helicopter. I think we can do some computer work at least I can while you rest and I'll fill you in."

"WE?""

"We were working on a joint F. B. I. and Driftwood County investigation, when someone put bombs in that damn helicopter and sabotaged the controls, I'll be damned if someone is going to get away with trying to kill us."

"I like the way you think. What do you know so far anything, Agent Summer?"

"Just so you know, I know your uncle was a notorious mobster, turned states' witness and is still under witness protection. I was surprised that they allowed your aunt(a sworn F. B. I. agent, who was supposed to just protect him) marry the man."

"Uncle Tommy's a charmer too, that's the only real similarity, I have to him."

"I've seen his picture, like I said you look alike but cut out the charm I'm not susceptible."

"Sorry, Agent Summer."

Dai consulted her computer I looked at it, but it all blurred together, until I had to shut my eyes for a moment to feel better and not so dizzy.

"Now that's over, I suspect that someone wanted either you, or your uncle dead."

"That was my conclusion too. My uncle was almost killed in Detroit, by a car bomb. My uncle also informed me, my aunt, Louise was not dead. Someone had faked her death to lure one of us to Detroit," I answered. ,

"Yes, you've told me that about a hundred times, but thanks again."

"Sorry. I must have been a handful."

"Handful? I've handled lots of men who were trouble."

"I bet you have," I commented.

"Listen Bullet this is your last warning, no more flirting, we have work to do and in order to do that you have to rest."

"But I'm not tired," I whined.

"Quit acting like a petulant child, shut your eyes! When you wake-up, maybe I'll have an update for you."

What could I do? I closed my eyes, thinking I'd only sleep for a half an hour. When I woke up it was the next day; but my head felt clearer and I felt much better. I was sure I could hobble out of this joint, if only I had some crutches and a hired car.

I glanced over the curtain was pulled between me and the patient in the next bed. I hobbled on my ankle, grabbing a pair of crutches, I spotted nearby; only to have my arm grabbed from behind.

"Did you think you were leaving without me Bullet? Think again."

"Of course not, but we need a rental car."

"All ready arranged .Now let me get dressed, we'll sign the against medical advice papers and blow this joint."

"I like how you think. So, we drive back to Driftwood?

"Yes," Dai said ,but something told me she was hiding something.

We left the building, both hobbling to where she said the car was, to my surprise at the wheel was Agent Paul Jones. Frankly, I suspected his name was changed from some other name .I just didn't like the man.

"Jones, "Dai acknowledged as we both climbed into the back seat of a luxury car.

"This isn't a standard issue car; where did you rent this from?" I asked.

"Your uncle sent this monstrosity." Jones complained. "He claims its bullet proofed and armor-plated.

"Can't you drive a luxury car, Agent Jones? I thought you wanted to work Secret Service detail," Dai needled, and I hid a laugh.

"Happy to do, whatever I'm told and sent to do, ma'am."

"Call me sir. That's what you'd call a superior you respected."

"Yes, sir," Jones groveled

"We're starving. Our first stop is a drive through Agent Jones." I requested.

"Find the nearest one and here's the money for it, my treat for everyone's breakfast. You're buying lunch, Bullet," Dai stated.

Jones ate while driving, one hand with an egg sandwich on his left hand ,the other his non-dominant hand his right ,on the wheel; while we finished our breakfast in the backseat. I found myself growing drowsy, even as Dai fired up her computer. I closed my eyes.

"Is he out? "Jones asked.

"I think so."

"There was another attempt on his uncle."

"How?" Dai asked.

"A car bomb again. His uncle changed his mind at the last minute and got an SUV to accommodate Bullet's aunt and daughter. I think he thought he'd drive them cross country. Now they are coming in on a flight in about eight hours from now to Denver."

"Is that safe?"

"They were escorted by law enforcement to the flight. Armed personal hired by Thomas Bullet are picking them up at the airport and will bring them to a safe house of Anne Bullet's choosing," Agent Jones explained.

"Why didn't you tell Bullet this when we got in the car?"

"He'd have insisted on driving to Denver and we're heading to Driftwood, He may have family difficulties, but we were set to investigate that train crash."

"You need to learn some etiquette Jonesy," I interjected, "A man's family is important especially to cops."

"I take it you heard the whole conversation? That doesn't excuse you calling me, Jonesy. Frankly, we don't know each other well enough for that, but I am sorry Bullet for not letting you know sooner. The good thing is your kid is safe."

"Golly, gee, thanks."

"Bullet, we have to work together can you put this behind us?"

"Did they discharge us with any pain pills? My head and ankle are killing me," I complained.

"In about an hour, we can make a stop for lunch; can you hold out until then?"

"I'll just take a nap, wake me when we get there," I answered.

"Cocky bastard, isn't he?"

"He maybe a small-town sheriff, but Bullet has a reputation for getting things solved," I heard Dai expound.

"We probably won't be in Driftwood long enough for that, it looks like sink holes took the train out."

"But why so many explosive materials on such a short train?" I asserted.

"Still listening in Bullet? You're only on this case as a courtesy. Believe me we have to fight the National Transportation Safety Board for jurisdiction. They want total control. All though I've got to say your people are incredible. Your Acting Sheriff Andrew Ambercrombie, his charming, pit-bull, sister, (your communication deputy) Penny Ambercrombie and of course our tactician, Agent Stone Summer are the reasons we even still on the case. Acting Sheriff Ambercrombie and Agent Stone were able to offer new information about sinkholes and about how they might have affected any sabotage of the train."

"If there was sabotage. That hasn't been proven yet, Agent Jones and there is still some speculation that the sinkholes could have caused the entire problem."

"How do you know that? I didn't tell you that!"

"I am the senior investigator; you should inform me of all the facts not those you choose to cherry pick."

"You had an injury... you were in the hospital!"

"I could probably let it go this time, but don't ever cross me again Jones. You are on thin ice don't cross me again," snarled Dai.

"The head agent Burke from the NTSB said we could remain in the game provided they get to check in with you, and my boss Agent Dia Summer, as we investigated, " Agent Jones stated looking back at me.

"Oh, so that's why I'm needed."

"Now listen here, Bullet!!"Agent Jones blustered.

"Don't get your shorts in a knot, Jonesy. Let's just work together and solve this problem, because like I said it's not just the sinkholes. I'm sure that between the three of them, we'll get some good information from the Ambercrombies and your agent. What has my brother, Blaze Trail been up to?"

"That's your brother? But he's an Indian and black."

"He prefers to be called indigenous."

"Are you sure he's telling the truth? He's like no Indian, I've ever seen. He could be lying and be a what is it called… a Pretendian? Maybe he's lying about being your what half- brother? I should investigate him," Jones sputtered.

"Maybe, you're lying about being an F. B. I agent maybe, I should investigate you," I said menacingly.

"I warned you, now Jones ,shut the hell up, before I write up your racist ass and you get posted to Greenland, "Dai shouted.

"You wouldn't!"

"Wouldn't I? You are a pain in the keester, Jones and this is a formal warning. I am writing you up."

"Please, I'm sorry, I apologise sir, ma'am."

"Pull over, I'm driving while you type and sign this report, I just made. We'll keep this between the three of us ,but Bullet and I will keep a written and signed account by you in case you slip again."

"I won't. It was slight slip. I've completed diversity training.

"What you get a D-minus?" I quipped, before I could stop myself.

"A guy makes one comment," muttered Jones.

"A boss makes another checkmark for sensitivity/ diversity refresher next month, that you better score an A on, and another black mark on his record, all of which are all adding up to dismal," Dai answered, and I swallowed a chuckle. but I also thought that bastard Jones better keep his racist crap to himself, or sooner or later we were going to come to blows.

I then thought about how many times had I let racist crap like this fly by me. Did that make me a racist? Probably, if I truly thought about it. I had no idea of the magnitude of racism, that my brother had gone through all of his life. I probably would never understand the extent of any of it; but I was going to try to stand up from now on and be an ally instead of being passive and letting people continue their racism. Was that enough? No, it probably wasn't. I heard of the abuse some sheriff deputies and other law enforcement had taken in my new state and I didn't want that for my brother or any other human being. God damn ,what a silly world we lived in. Two steps forward ,six steps back, that's what it seemed like, when it came to civil rights.

My cell rang and when I looked at it, I found Andrew's name on.

"Andrew? I can barely hear you."

"Boss, apparently the NTSB tried to call the F.B. I. ,but they haven't been able to reach Agent Summers is she there?"

I knew this code; it was do you want them to talk to her?

I motioned to Dai that it was for both of us and she had Jones pull the car over.

"I hope the signal will be good. I'll try to video call you Andrew."

Seconds later, despite the previous low signal, we were now fully connected. I held the phone up, so, Dia could see. Andrew introduced the National Transportation Board investigator, Kathleen Kristiansen.

"She takes over from Philip Ashby."

Then Kathleen came on camera and I gasped and pulled the phone so it was directly on me, not on Dia.

"Hello, coz, fancy meeting you again this way," she laughed.

"I knew you worked for the government. but I wasn't aware it was the NTBS and you are spouting a new name ."

"Yes, dad doesn't exactly brag, does he?"

"Uncle Bennie is quiet, unless he's talking about police work. but come on coz, your last name changed too."

"That is recent and dad doesn't know that Kasper and I eloped to Vegas last week."

"He's met your husband, Kasper Kristiansen. though?"

"Yes, but he has no idea we were dating. Kasper is a criminal lawyer."

"I can see how that will go over like gangbusters."

"Not you, too!

"No, if he treats you right and you're happy, I won't judge his profession."

"Thank you Gee. By the way I've met your brother, Blaze. He seems like a great guy, and I'm going to call him my cousin, even though we are unrelated by blood."

"Blaze is a great guy. You better break it gently to Uncle Bennie about your wedding then, and maybe don't mention Blaze yet. I'm not sure how happy he would be about my brother and I don't want him disturbing Blaze. Now back to business, what conclusions have you reached Kathleen about our train crash? This is Agent Dai Summers by the way and Dai, this is my cousin, Kathleen Kristiansen."

"Your cousin, wow isn't this a family affair, ha-ha. The crash itself was cause by a sinkhole near the tracks the ones you and Andrew discovered. Philip tried to report this to you, Agent Summers, but he was cockblocked by that Jones character. He got so frustrated he asked for a transfer and so they appointed me lead investigator in his place. Philip felt that Jones was censoring any calls from him and keeping it from you Agent Summers."

"You son of a bitch. Who the heck do you think you are?" Dai erupted at Jones.

"You were injured and I was only doing my job."

"Your job was to keep your superior informed and in the loop. You did none of that."

"I did what I think was best."

"I have reported this to your superiors; I hope this doesn't reflect bad on you, Agent Summers. I did tell them that Philip found you very professional and so did he, but your underling, Jones was abusive and unprofessional, and that we are unable to work with him. I'm sure you'll be getting a call soon from your bosses. Sorry about that, hope I didn't create problems."

"Don't be sorry. Jones was well aware that he was skating on thin ice and my bosses are not enthused with his unprofessionalism."

"I'm sorry I was doing my job."

"Shut-up Jones!!"Dai said then said, "Sorry about that Agent Kristiansen."

"Kathleen in present company, except Jones, he can call me Agent Kristiansen. Now further about this train crash. The train was rigged with explosives that probably would have gone off in Denver where it was routed."

"Are you saying it was terrorism? What about the explosives have they gone off?" Dai and I asked simultaneously

"Andrew found them before they could be set off. We were lucky enough to have someone with the highest bomb tec experience available immediately, namely your brother, Blaze Trail. He says learned it serving his country. I suspect he was in the marines given his tattoos, probably some elite force."

"Don't speculate if Blaze wants us to know, he'll reveal it," I cautioned.

"He's kind of like my uncles and my dad. He's a man of few words; he'd fit right into a family gathering."

"Blaze is at that."

"Back to the bombs…"Kathleen said.

"Bombs as in plural?" I demanded to know.

"Yes, there were four! We were lucky they didn't all go off with the fire and the destruction caused by the sinkholes. The fire near the rear of the train was caused by a smaller bomb without as much force as the other three we discovered."

"So, a big investigation?"

"Yes, and we welcome some help from your force as well, as Agent Dai Summers' people as long as Jones doesn't participate. Frankly, the other Agent Summers is a sweetheart."

"I'll tell my sister you said that," Agent Summers commented.

"Sisters? Of course, I can see that now. I was thinking, maybe cousins, but despite you having dark and her light and different eye colours, you are very similar looking. Sorry, that's a little forward a Bullet trait I'm trying to overcome, sorry. I'll see you in person tomorrow. I'm sure."

"You will, now I'll let you talk to your cousin, Sheriff Bullet."

"Hi again, Gee .If I'm going to meet with and investigate this with you all I'll have to stay in town but there isn't any housing everything is full with relatives or people displaced in town and other personnel. I don't suppose you have space for me and Kasper?"

"Kasper is in town?"

"We were on our honeymoon when I got the call, and Kasper insisted that this was the break of my career and I needed to go."

"I'm staying at my Uncle Tommy's...," I began.

"Not thee, Uncle Tommy," she asked sounding surprised.

"The very one. He has a security detail protecting me there. Someone called said Aunt Louise was dead and tried to lure either Uncle Tommy, and myself/ or, both of us."

"Good grief, but Aunt Louise is dead, isn't she? She died a long with your little girl. What is it a couple of years ago. By the way I'm so sorry, Gee. I should have reached out long ago."

"Didn't Uncle Bennie, or the uncles tell you? I am so sorry, Kathleen. They were both in witness protection. The uncles knew you can't keep secrets from them.

I had to pretend they were dead to protect both of them and then this hoax happens ,just when they are on there way home, and someone blew up Uncle Tommy's car."

"But you're not even where ever she was. Your helicopter crashed. Was that sabotage too?"

"Possibly it was Uncle Tommy's helicopter."

"I heard one of my colleagues is at the site investigating the crash of that helicopter; so, I guess will know soon enough."

"There's room at the other small guest house for you and Kasper. I'm sure Uncle Tommy wouldn't mind."

"Are you sure? I mean he's your uncle, not mine."

"I could call him and ask."

"Please do that, I wouldn't want to impose, cousin."

"I'll text you the details, once I talk to him. Glad to have you in town, Kathleen."

'It will be nice to see you, too. Andrew your acting sheriff, has sent someone to drive you, back. He doesn't trust Jones. Stay put until he comes."

"Who is he sending?"

"Errol Ward."

I quickly texted Uncle Tommy ,about my cousin, needing accommodation.

My phone beeped; speak of the devil it was Uncle Tommy.

"See you soon, Kathleen. I have to take another call, coz. Bye."

A few minutes after talking to Uncle
Tommy, I phoned Blaze to get him to get the
keys. His bodyguard went with him ,while
he retrieved the keys Blaze then presented
to Kathleen who thanked me by text.

Jones now sat in the backseat, and I was
waiting in the front seat with Dai at the
wheel . Jones looked in a filthy mood. He
probably realized he was close to be fired; I
determined.

My phone rang again, interrupting my
thoughts once again. I put it up to my ear
speaking in whispers so Jones wouldn't
overhear.

"Uncle Tommy I just hung up with you,
what's up?"

"Are you sitting down?"

"I take it this is bad news."

"I was looking it to some information, to see
if I could figure who s behind all of this the
bombing and the lies of your Aunt Louise's
death."

"Are you telling me you found something,.
or is it someone out?"

"I had my own man ,look at the evidence a rush job ,and he assured me that it was definitely a bomb, as I suspected .I can't say that this person is connected to this, but it seems like this could be a clue. I'd like to known where these people were during the last week."

"Who are you talking about?"

"It's a bit of a story. They needed some information about an inmate and who comes to their rescue? You guessed it, it's Derek Chittwood. He got them some information they needed from a serial killer. He played the serial killer and the guy told Derek where he hid the bodies and how he committed the crime. Derek testified, the system commuted his sentence to time served (given that he was a former cop and had been a model prisoner.)"

"Son of a bitch! Why did they notifying me, his victim? When did all this go down?"

"He's been free for the last four weeks and that's not all."

"What?"

"There's more, Gina was released early. She gets to perform 500 hours of community service and report to her parole officer for the next five years."

"Gina escaped! Didn't they hold that against her?"

"No, seems they didn't. Gina hasn't reported to her parole officer, either and no one seems to be looking for her, but me."

"That can't be right, you can't just not show up for your parole officer and not be looked for. Do you think they are together, again?"

"It might be possible. Derek hasn't check in either.

"Shit! What is wrong with the court system?"

"You must see lots of injustice on both sides, being a cop, Gee. You know this isn't new. We have to stop them."

"Gina apologised to me. She wouldn't help Derek."

"Then he's kidnapped her, because my sources believe they are together."

"I can't understand, what did I do to deserve to have him in my life? Frankly, I thought this was over when he went to jail. I still can't believe any of it. The man used to be a cop, was my superior why would he use bombs?"

"Why did he try to kill you in the first place? The man is in love with Gina and thinks if he gets rid of you, she'll turn to him. I think Stella-Marie is in danger; he'll try to grab for Gina.

"He probably thinks he can make Stella-Marie hate you, and accept him as daddy, since you told her mother she was dead."

"What am I supposed to do? How do we protect Aunt Louise and Stella- Marie?"

"Are you deaf? I've got guards on them. They are safe as safe as Fort Knox. I'm more worried about you. Derek Chittwood wants you dead and he still has law enforcement buddies who will help him. so don't trust anyone except people you know are loyal."

"I trust my people."

"Don't trust any new recruits then. Derek could have had this plan in place, a long time."

"What if it's not him? It could be someone I arrested."

'Get your head out of your you know what, boy. Most likely the enemy is someone who knows you well and that is Derek Chittwood, he hates you! He and that evil ex-wife of yours tried to end you and only didn't succeed because your best friend caught them. Now he's manipulated the system to be free from jail do you think he won't come for you."

"We can't let him get a hold of my daughter, my Stella-Marie."

"You are too trusting of that witch. Gina probably is behind all of this the only thing she cares about is hurting you. "I hired guards to protect them and get them safe to you. I've also hired more to protect them once they reach Driftwood."

"But what about Chittwood? We need to find him. I'm going to have to ask the F. B. I for help."

"I'll continue to use my contacts to ferret the snake out, but yes, I think you should reach out to Special Agent Dai Summer. Don't trust her underling, that Jones, though, and tell your cousin about the danger. My sources say that man Jones is wishy-washy and an ass-kisser. I don't knowhow you can be both, but it seems his made his career of both of those things. I hope your cousin and her husband are happy staying in the cottage. I've sent some staff to make it more cozy and have the fridge filled with easy serve meals as well as numbers for delivery services. I hope that way their honeymoon can continue despite the interruption."

"Can you come home Uncle Tommy? I'd feel better if you were safe here."

"Of course, I'll be there soon, my wife is there too and I'll see your child and Aunt Louise get there safely. We have some things to discuss and I've got something important to tell you."

"Can't you speak now?"

"No, I have to go one my sources are beckoning me. We'll talk as soon as I'm home. Until then be watchful and stay safe. I can't lose you. I want you to know you are like a son to me."

"I love you too, Uncle Tommy."

"Now don't get all mushy on me. Time's a ticking I have to go and check my car for bombs before I drive away."

"We'll talk soon."

"Yes, we will my boy."

I hung up concerned and called Errol.

"Are you almost to me?" I asked.

"Should be there with in the next half-hour," he answered.

"Let's have dinner tonight. I'd like to get to now you a little better."

"You got it Dai, if you don't mind eating with my daughter," :I whispered, "Keep an eye out would you Agent Summer. I'm going to take a nap,"

She nodded. I closed my eyes and was asleep within minutes.

~0~

Chapter 9 – Back to Driftwood

I exited the car only to be confronted by the mayor, Gertrude Fines.

"G. I need a word can you come back to my office?"

"There's a lot going on as you can see," I said gesturing towards Agent Summer.

"I wouldn't be addressing you after your recent helicopter crash injuries if it wasn't so urgent."

I excused myself and ushered Dai into my office with Andrew.

"I'll be back soon and then we can discuss the train derailment updates," I said then excused myself and went to Gertrude's nearby office

"What's up Gert?"

"G, I am tapped into a source that the rest of the council doesn't have. I heard your attacker , possibly Chittwood and your ex-wife are on the loose. They've been released prematurely and that your ex-wife is missing; so, how are you holding up?"

"I'm fine and I have someone looking into that for me."

"Your aunt and your little girl were supposed to come home; are they safe?"

"My uncle has hired guards to protect them."

"Glad to hear that, but you know Melanie Halton will use this, so be on your guard. She tried to use my daughter dropping out of college to become an actress, against me in the last election. Karoline first movie comes out in a week. She's not the lead but she's not an extra either. I'm so proud of her"

"Wow , good for Karoline, Thank-you for the heads up, Gert. Was there anything else?"

"Bad news for your election. Melanie Halton's son, Dick Richards has moved back to Driftwood."

"His name is Dick Richards?" I chuckled.

"You can laugh all you want, but he worked in California as a cop, and not just a cop ,but a supervisor too."

"His name isn't the same as Melanie's, I'd never have guessed."

She married his father ,the late Richard Richards who was a deputy chief killed in the line of duty. Dickie has had lots of experience and Melanie's got the other council members backing him."

"I've done a good job, even when I've been injured. I've got the job done. I think they'll back me."

"They are going to use that against you. Melanie has been insinuating that you brought the crime from Chicago."

"They can't have fallen for that."

"They claim that Driftwood was a quiet city before you came."

"Sure, that's why almost the whole police force was killed before I even started work."

"You may have to remind them of that. The other thing is that your uncle running for mayor is not good, I don't mind the competition per se, but I have the experience, your uncle doesn't ..Isn't there anyway you could convince him to run for deputy mayor instead?"

"I don't know."

'I know I'm putting you in a difficult position, but this is the best for Driftwood and I promise I'll drop hints about all the crime you've cleaned up."

"I'll try."

"That's all I can ask. Now if you can wrap up this trail derailment ,in a big red bow, you can beat Melanie's son."

"I'll try. We are close to wrapping this up. Anything else on your mind?'

"Just that we are friends Gee, and I support you one hundred percent for re-election. You have been the best sheriff we've ever had, but I can't begin to tell you how your uncle's campaign is really not working for either of us! He's causing division in the community and my campaign manager assures me he's not going to be mayor. Is there anything I can offer him that he will back off?"

"I'm sorry Gert. I didn't even know he was running, until recently."

"I have sway with two thirds of the council. We could appoint him deputy mayor, if he backs me. Tell him to see the polls himself! He can't win ,but for the good of Driftwood I'm willing to back his play as deputy mayor."

"What is there in it ,for you?"

"Tell him I care about Driftwood, and if Tom continues, he'll divide the populace vote and then Jared Brentwood will win. Jared wants to develop all the land outside of Driftwood. He's secretly talking about expropriation, just so he can build a huge resort for his donors He keeps insisting that Driftwood will benefit in tourist dollars. It isn't true; he's just giving them a sweetheart deal. They'll lease the land for a hundred years and we can't get out of the deal for at least thirty years without paying millions of dollars in penalties. They'll believe it that because he's a Democrat, or had vacillated to Republican? People question every word you. your uncle or I say, but Jared can do no wrong."

"Can't you just tell people this?"

"Oh, Gee ,that's what I like about you, you are so naïve. People only hear what they want to hear. Jared's telling people who will vote for him, that your uncle and I are the enemy. Apparently, we are the reason that Driftwood has areas that have declined in value."

"I'll let my uncle know, but I can't promise anything."

"That's all I ask. This is my new phone number ,only give it out to your uncle. If you want to reach me, call my old number,"

"Is this a burner phone number?"

"I promise it's nothing nefarious, at least not at my part. I've just found out that Brentwood may have tapped my phone, so, I'm careful to who and what I'm revealing the information."

"That's illegal. Do you want me to arrest him?"

"No, let it go. He'll hang himself. I plan on reveal some campaign details all lies of course, but he'll fall for it; just you watch."

"I like how you think Gert. I wouldn't want you as an enemy."

"I don't think that will ever happen. You were great hire. Gee and I told them that when they showed me your resume. The thing is you are an even better person and friend. A person would be crazy to throw that away."

"Aw shucks, ma'am."

'Get out of here, idiot, and go get some work done," Gert said gruffly, but with a smile to take out the sting.

"I'll get my uncle to get back to you," I promised.

"Thank- you Gee. See you later."

I walked back to my office, my head killing me. I hoped there was still that bottle of aspirin in my desk drawer. I could use a bottle full, but of course I'd follow the label.

I also had tons of paperwork that needed completion, before I could leave and see my little girl. I missed having her around everyday, and the fact that Luis Cervantes had taken that away from me ,grated on me/\. I was secretly glad, he was dead, so, I didn't have to face down my other nature ,who might have taken the situation in his own hands and not done the right thing given the threat to my child and aunt.

Now I was faced with that again would I keep that in check if Derek Chittwood was behind all this? Of course, I would, I reasoned, but a small part of me, wasn't as sure.

~0~

Chapter 10 - Uncle Tommy Never Learned to Played Ball

Stepping into my office, I breathed a sigh of relief. No one was waiting there. I glanced over the mountains of paperwork on my desk and propping up my leg (on a spare chair) I began to read. Two hours later I'd barely made a dint in all the work and my eyes were beginning to swim.

I needed to shut my eyes for a half an hour, but with my luck someone would barge in. I locked my office door and laid down. Five minutes wouldn't hurt I thought. I woke up to someone tapping my shoulder. Alarmed, I threw open my eyes and saw the culprit.

"Uncle Tommy? How did you get here so fast?"

"I'm surprised you are not asking me, how I got into your office."

"Okay, I'll ask, even if I 'll probably regret it."

"Skeleton key. Opens a lot of old fashion locks."

"Memo to Penny. Please order a locksmith to put a better lock on my office door." I said into my phone.

"Your aunt and your sweet little girl, are installed at my place. There are two 24- hour guards and they'll only allow you, or myself near them."

"What about Blaze?"

"If you would like to take him to see them, he'll be allowed but only with supervision."

"Don't you trust Blaze?"

"I'm protecting them. Whoever is behind this won't be able to blackmail Blaze, or anyone else to get to see them."

"Not bad Uncle Tommy."

"What was the mayor talking to you about?"

"How could you know about that? You weren't in town then, were you? That was six hours ago." I said looking at my computer clock."

"No, but that doesn't mean ,I didn't have someone watching the town. Did she offer you a Bulldog?"

"A what? Why would she offer me a dog?"

Uncle Tommy chuckled," It's not a dog. You got to start thinking and acting like a native son, or they'll turn you out first chance they get. A Colorado Bulldog is a drink. I think the Russians brought it here. Take a splash of cola, mix 1 ounce of vodka, 1 ounce of coffee liqueur, 2 ounces of cream (or milk), and 2 ounces of Coca-Cola. served with ice."

"Gert didn't offer me a drink. She wanted to tell me that Melanie Halton has swayed the council into backing her son Dick and that you were running for mayor."

"There's something fishing about that guy, Dick. If he was so successful why come back to Driftwood? No offence nephew."

"Yes, I wondered that, too, but if Gert tells me he was in a supervisor position., I believe her. That would give him prestige with the voters."

"Not to worry, sonny boy, they'll see you are the best choice. That can't be all Gertie wanted from you."

"Seriously, aren't you worried that running for mayor your enemies will find you. I mean one picture and they can find you. Running for and being the mayor has pictures" on the internet.

"You've been using the device that detects bugs, right?" Uncle Tommy asked conspiratorially.

"Yes, I checked this morning, now how are you going to stop the pictures?"

"Our friend has given me new AI software that alters my image. Either it makes it faded , or changes the way I look. No one will see the real me."

"That sounds impossible."

"Our friend is known for the impossible."

"I guess that will work nicely, then. I'm still worried about what Gert said to tell you. She said you running for mayor will divide the populace vote and then Jared Brentwood will win. Jared wants to develop all the land outside of Driftwood. Gert lost the

nomination with the Democrats and s
running as an independent against him"

"I've heard, but tell me more."

"He's secretly talking about expropriation so
he can build a huge resort, for his donors
and insisting that Driftwood will benefit in
tourist dollars and your property is one of
the ones he wants. Of course, he's lying he
wants to give the spa a sweetheart deal.
They'll lease the land for a hundred years
and we can't get out of the deal for at least
thirty years without paying millions of
dollars in penalties."

"Why does she think the populace will fall
for that?"

"She thinks because they'll believe because
he's a Democrat he is lying. She 's willing
to back you as deputy mayor if you just step
down and don't run against her."

Uncle Tommy started laughing and almost
fell to the floor then he pulled himself
together and stated, "She maybe right about
how crooked Jared is and that people will
believe a Democrat. Even though Gertie's
running as an independent they know she's a
Democrat. I got to tell you there are a lot of
people out there pulling for change and that

means another party. Now I'm running as a Republican and I'm going to win so she need not worry she can be my deputy mayor."

"Uncle Tommy! "I admonished.

"What? If it's supposed to be good enough for me, why isn't it good enough for Sweet Gertie?"

"You're not going to play ball are you Uncle Tommy?"

"Would you? Besides I never had time to play ball as a kid. I was too busy running numbers."

"Uncle Tommy, I'm sorry, I pressured you."

"It's okay kid, I understand. Jared Brentwood tried to take me down. It's a matter of principal now."

"What did he do?"

"He tried to get me to hire two of his spies, and they planted bugs ,even though I turned them away. He also tried to tap my cell phone ,but I have the finest up to date spyware. He couldn't."

"Am I in danger from that? Do you want me to arrest him, Uncle Tommy?"

"No, your cell phone has been upgraded. I had it upgraded when you were at that clinic. I also had your station upgraded with some techs. No one can spy on you here, either."

"Who could do that? Not her?"

"The very same, just because she doesn't exist on paper, doesn't mean I can't get access to Paris' tech."

"Should you be saying her first name?"

"No, but her tech is supposed to keep any listening impossible. I won't mention her again."

"She's doing well?"

"Yes, and her child is happy too."

"Good.

"I need to check in with my campaign office after I leave here but I've assigned two men to watch you and Blaze."

"Uncle Tommy don't be ridiculous. I'm that Sheriff how will that look?"

"How will it look if someone kills you, while you're going about doing your job and you get killed, leaving your daughter in a custody fight, with her criminal mother and me?"

"I'm sorry Uncle Tommy, but I really must put my foot down."

"So, shall I'll just hire someone? You'll never even notice that they are following you and I'll still have my way."

"I'm not happy about this but you already hired someone didn't you?"

"I'm not either, Gunner, but yes of course I have hired a man you'll never spot him he's an old spy and he'll protect you for the price I'm paying. I also hired his buddy for Blaze so we'll all be safe. We'll get through this and nail the culprit and if it's Derek Chittwood, he better hope I don't find him."

"I am the law Uncle Tommy let me apprehend him and put him back I prison where he belongs."

"Fine but I'm still going to help."

"I wouldn't have it any other way. Now I'm about to head home to see my little girl and my favorite aunt."

"See you soon then."

"Bye, Uncle Tommy," I said hanging up.

~0~

Chapter 11 - Prepare for Disaster, Recover Faster

I checked over my car thoroughly, and didn't find any bombs; but I did find a tracking device. I spotted a UPS truck at the corner and decided to have a little fun, placing it under the rear bumper.

I was really beginning to think that the bombs had been placed by Derek. Chittwood, or his henchmen. He really hated me. Why? Other than him wanting my ex-wife I'd never given him cause, but then she had managed to convince him to kill me. She was a very convincing liar. She could have convinced him of anything. She almost fooled me again, when I saw her earlier this year, just had a magnetism it was hard for any man to resist. I had fooled myself into thinking Derek had been the first one she cheated on me with. After she was convicted (along with Derek Chittwood of trying to kill me) different men contacted me. They told me Gina was a siren, and they were sorry for fooling around with my wife. Yet, I had believed her earlier this year, yet again that she had changed. Some part of me still wanted to believe in her. They were correct the woman was a siren.

Uncle Tommy insisted that all the women in her family, were the same and should have neon signs around their necks screaming siren. Even her little sister, Luna had Andrew wrapped around her little finger, he insisted loudly, when I protested. He then stated that although Andrew wanted to date Luna, they still hadn't formally acknowledged they were dating and Luna was the good sister. The rest of them used their wicked wiles even more to get exactly what they wanted and more he continued.

I know he sounded like a misogynist, but he insisted I was the naïve one, that there were women in the world who just exude the it-factor, and they are totally unstoppable. Let

me backtrack here, Gina so far was the only
totally wicked one, but I was being careful
given that Gina had fooled me. I wouldn't
trust her sisters either except for Luna and
maybe Loretta. I'd had to promise Uncle
Tommy, so he'd drop the you are so naïve
talk, but did I really believe they were
trouble? Why no!

Yet, here we were again and Derek was
trying to kill me again, probably on Gina's
behalf. Where had Derek learned to build
bombs and plant tracking devices? Did
someone give him a crash course in prison?
Of course they did Chittwood was nothing,
if he wasn't persuasive.

I suddenly looked around; I was almost to
my new abode. Talk about distracted driving
if I had seen another driver doing this, I
would have given him a warning or perhaps
a ticket. I admonished myself. There, there
was the turnoff. I drove down a driveway
only to be stopped at a new guard tower.

I rolled down my window to two security
guards.

"Name please, I dentification and reason for being here?" demanded the one in charge.

"I am Sheriff G. Bullet and I live here now. Didn't Uncle Tommy tell you?"

"Sorry your uncle insists on certain protocols, or we are fired. We are still going to ask you to produce valid government identification every time. As we already asked Special Agent Dai Summers. I understand she's your guest, but she has been okayed by Thomas Bullet."

"Dai's here already?" Fine, far be it, that I get you fired, because then I'd have to hire you as officers, would I?"I joked, but the security guard smiled and seemed to look hopeful, like I was going to make an offer as I offered him my identification.

"That was a joke you know, right?" I commented when the one officer still stared at me.

"Yes sir, Sheriff Bullet. Proceed down the drive you will be asked for your identification before they let you go to the door, so, keep it handy, "cautioned the other guard.

"Right you are."

I could see that Uncle Tommy had stepped up security more than the two gate officers and identification requirements, it looked like there was now an electrified fence around the property and I could see men roaming the place with attack dogs. Was Stella-Marie safe to play outside? I'd have to talk to Uncle Tommy about this.

I was followed to in the house by a security guard ,who only left after seeing Uncle Tommy.

"Is this going to happen every time?"

"What the security checks or your shadow that came in the house?"

"All of it."

"You know what they say prepare for disaster, recover faster."

"There's no disaster. No only my car blowing up after being lured to Detroit and then your helicopter exploding. You are lucky to be alive my boy; so, I say all my precautions will keep us all that way. Now that your home I'm off will speak later."

Uncle Tommy then left and I looked around wondering where Aunt Louise and my daughter was.

My query was answered by a devilish, whirlwind ,of arms and legs ,who ran across the room and jumped into my arms crying, "Daddy! You're home! I missed you!"

"I have missed you too my little pumpkin, light of my life."

"Oh daddy. I'm not a pumpkin! Right Aunt Louise? Right Dai?"

"That's right," Dai answered, "You are positively old."

"I'm not old! You're funny Dai."

"You are a big girl now. Not a baby." Aunt Louise corrected.

"You are my baby forever, but you are getting to be such a big girl. I hate that I missed so much of that." I stated, "Shall I call you a squash, or an orange then?"

I just laughed when she nodded and smiled wickedly.

"I like your new friend," Stella – Marie whispered.

"That's good she's staying for supper."

"I know Stella- Marie answered rolling her eyes, then almost jumping up and down she cried, I'm so excited I get to see my friends tomorrow."

I raised an eyebrow and looked at Aunt Louise.

"Stella-Marie needs her schooling and interaction with other children. All the other kids are being bused to the Teardrop Canyon School over in Teardrop Canyon. You know it's not safe for them to be in downtown Driftwood and Covid had been very bad for the children. She wears a mask. She'll be safe; but will you at the Sheriff station?" Aunt Louise asked.

Dai said, "We'll keep safe and Stella-Marie needs her friends.", but then she excused herself to the bathroom realizing she had no say in this. I didn't want to argue in front of Stella-Marie, but I was worried. I must have conveyed my feelings through my face because Aunt Louise said," I've enrolled her in Teardrop Canyon Elementary. She'll be very safe they have an officer on duty.

You've met them since you had to send another officer there because of the overflow of children."

"Oh, yes, the resource officer, Rebecca Crawford."

"She's good at her job, correct?"

"Then all is well, Stella-Marie goes to grade one, tomorrow."

"Wow, Stella-Marie are you excited? I'm driving you but you can take the bus the next day" I commented.

"Of course, I'm excited but I can already read so I guess I have to work on some adding and what was that other word Aunt Louise ,when you take numbers away?"

"Subtraction."

"Yes, that."

"I didn't know you could read. Do you want to read to me?" I asked.

"Can I daddy?"

Stella-Marie ran to what I assume was her new temporary bedroom and came running back with a book.

The title was Paper Bag Princess by Robert
Munch, a Canadian author, I wasn't familiar
with, but the story was just what I wanted
for my daughter. The heroine was the paper
bag princess.

Stella-Marie read clearly hardly stumbling
over any of the words and when she had any
hesitation, we sounded them out.

I was amazed for her age; she read very
well. Dare I say, she was advanced for her
age? I wanted to take the credit, but I knew
that as she had done for me Aunt Louise had
taught my daughter how to read. The next
generation benefited from Aunt Louise.

Aunt Louise was right, I was being extra
cautious, Stella-Marie needed to interact
with other children and a resource officer
would keep her safe. For Pete's sake she
participated in active shooter drills in
kindergarten she knew what to do. I was
being an overprotective father, but still I
worried.

After a lovely early dinner together with Dai
and Aunt Louise, I then I drove back to my
sheriff's office accompanied by Dai to take
some meetings on the train derailment. Dai
was charming and flirting with me. She

seemed to like me to maybe when this derailment issue was over, we could go on a date? No, she'd probably be gone by then but until then maybe I'd invite her more often for dinner with my family. It was midnight when I got home and then by the time I got through the checkpoints it was 12;30 a.m...

I went to sleep as soon as my head hit the pillow, my alarm set for 6 a.m. I figured if I got some work done, I could then drive Stella-Marie, to school for her first day.

~0~

Chapter 12 - School Days, Adult Play Days

T he day dawned, a lovely blue sky with

sunshine, bright and warm ,on this end of-August day. I dropped Stella-Marie off, to her cheery cries of hello to her old classmates who were overjoyed to see her .She'd be okay. I noted that her old friend, Helena Scioli was at her side and chatting, gleefully. I had a word with the resource officer, Rebecca Crawford. I was surprised to see it wasn't her, instead it seemed that it was one of the new hires, Karl Antonov. This was my first time meeting him but he seemed capable. He promised to watch over Stella-Marie and I was satisfied.

I was sure Stella-Marie was happy, that's all that mattered, besides the fact that she was safe. So she'd go to school, socialize and learn.

As for me I was back to my office, knee-deep in more paperwork until the bell rang at four. At least that's what I thought, but you know about the best laid plans.

I worked through the morning and as it neared 11 o'clock, I started feeling hungry and thought I'd take an early lunch. My phone rang and Daiyiilah asked, "I'm taking a two-hour lunch want to join me?"

"Where ?"I asked intrigued ,by the sound in her voice.

"Meet me at my room at the inn at the corner? It's room 234."

She flirted with me before ,but this sounded like she was offering something, or was I reading her wrong?"

"Your room, not a restaurant?"

"Don't be so dense. Do I have to spell it out for you? We both need to let off some steam. I'm a woman, you're a man. Yada, yada, yada."

"I'll be there with bells on." I answered.

"It holds bells, this I have to see," Dai
laughed hanging up.

Dai answered the door in a red bra and some
sexy panties which I just wanted to pull off
the minute, I saw her; but I let her take the
lead.

I started kissing her the minute, I was
through the door. Dai was quicker, she shut
the door with her one hand and undid my
pants with the other. I pulled off her
underwear and we shimmied unto the bed.
She pulled off my drawers and my shirt, as I
undid her bra. Her breasts were glorious, full
round and perfectly proportioned. I grew
even hotter, starring at them

Legs entwined, fingers touching
everywhere, whispers, and then sighs
exchanged ,as we climaxed over and over
again.

I thought she'd compliment me, or
something, or at least make plans for us to
be together again; but she just got up quickly
and took a shower. I got up to join her, but
she waved me away. I took a shower after
her, and when I came out Dai said, "That
was fun, but you're not feeling committed
to me, are you? I mean were both adults and

we don't get attached just because we sleep with a friend, do we?"

"No, of course not, friends with benefits. Right?"

"That's right. I'm glad we're on the same page. You had me worried there for a minute with that puppy dog look you gave me."

"You mean the hound dog look? I was just appreciate our time together, but as you said friends with benefits."

"We'll get together some time when we are both stressed again," Dai commented

"Yes, sure It's back to work for me and you."

I looked at my watch; damn, I needed to get back to the office and get some work done, before leaving to get Stella-Marie. But I really wasn't sure about this, *friends with benefits*. Was I that kind of man? Even if I wasn't ready to move on from my beloved second wife, Tina.

~0~

Chapter 13 - Former Cops Don't Play Fair

I looked at my watch, it was almost three thirty, I really should leave now to get to the school for Stella-Marie.

I collected my paperwork putting in a neat pile and told Penny, I'd be back in a couple of hours.

Nearing the school, I heard the bell ring and saw children were leaving the school. I scanned the crowd, searching for Stella-Marie, or perhaps one of her classmates, like her new/old friend, Helena Scioli. There was Helen, but no Stella-Marie. What was taking her so long? I watched as more kids came out, but again, no Stella-Marie.

I was getting scared, where was my daughter? I charged into the school and was stopped momentarily by my resource officer, Rebecca Crawford, who had switched back from Karl Antonov. Why was she not there this morning and now she was here and Karl was not? Rebecca explained she had a dental appointment and Karl had offered to fill in this morning. I told her next time to run it by me. Then she told me she had not seen my daughter all afternoon.

I scurried to her classroom and find it locked. My heart was pounding and my mouth was dry ,as ,I struggled for composure. Where was my daughter? It had to be all right! Stella-Marie had to be safe. They had her in the office; I told myself.

I went to the main office Stella-Marie wasn't there. I found myself charging into the principal's office.

"Sorry, Principal Gordon I did try to stop him," the administrative assistant said.

"I beg your pardon; did we have an appointment Sheriff Bullet?"

"I was waiting for my daughter Stella-Marie, but she never came out."

"But we received a call from you saying that your brother Carl was picking her up. At the last recess. Carl Bullet picked her up. He must have picked her up, Stella-Marie didn't come in from recess."

"I don't have a brother Carl and my brother that I do have, isn't listed as a person that can pick up Stella-Marie. Don't you have teachers on the yard? There are only certain people who can pick her up and this stranger wasn't one! Who did you let pick up my daughter? Where was that teacher while this man took my daughter?"

"Sheriff Bullet, do not use that tone with me! We used protocol and you have no jurisdiction in Teardrop Canyon!"

"Principal Gordon, I beg to differ; your sheriff, Sheriff Butler is out on sick leave and I'm covering both jurisdictions. Now despite the fact I have a crisis going on in Driftwood with the train derailment. I really have no time to deal with your shenanigans, right now, believe me we will get into this later. I have to put an Amber Alert for my daughter and hope that someone hasn't harmed her. When I have finished, I expect to talk to the person/ teacher that turned her over to this Carl. I need a description of this person immediately," I said my voice low, but deadly.

My mind turned to how selfish I was to spend time with Dai, when my daughter was in real danger; but I decide to beat myself up later I had to find Stella-Marie.

The administrative assistant standing at the door, said "I didn't know. I didn't know he wasn't who he said he was! He showed me identification that said he was Carl Bullet and he was old enough to be your uncle. He then went on the yard and I didn't see him again."

"What did this man look like give me a description!!," I demanded.

"He was about six feet, close to your height, I think. He was white and had dark brown hair and brown eyes. He really seemed nice. I didn't know that he wasn't your uncle."

With Principal Gordon still muttering in my ear (and protesting her innocence as well as her non-culpability) I took down the information and managed to draw a rough sketch with a piece of paper and pencil the administrative secretary Clovis Brown. I then wrote all the description of the kidnapper down and called Andrew and put out a statewide BOLO on my daughter and her kidnapper. Even thinking those words shook me to the core. It wasn't Derek Chittwood in person who had kidnapped Stella -Marie, so, she was in grave danger from whoever he had hired. Was Stella-Marie scared, was she crying for me? What had I done? Why hadn't I prevented this abduction?

Dai came on the line and said that she would make sure the F. B. I would put out a BOLO as well, to keep her from being taken across state lines. I bit my tongue, so, I didn't tell her that I shouldn't have been with her when my daughter was in danger. I was the worst father in the world! How could I have put my own desires before my daughter? What was wrong with me? Stella-Marie had to be all right. I'd make it up to her if only she was safe.

"Hang in there, Sheriff Bullet we will find her," Dai insisted.

I said a quick thank-you cutting her off and then said a quick goodbye, I then called Uncle Tommy

"Uncle Tommy, I need as many men that you can spare. Someone has taken Stella-Marie and I suspect it was Derek, behind the kidnapping but I haven't got a picture of the suspect yet. Stay on the line while I speak with the principal and her teacher and see if I can get more of a description of the culprit that I can sketch"

"Son of a bitch I thought my guy would keep her safe where is my guy? Let me call him while I place you on hold."

A few seconds later Uncle Tommy said, "He's not answering let me use 'Find Me'."

"Normally I would make fun of that, but right now I'm saying thank God, you have a guy on her and you can find him maybe he's saved Stella-Marie."

"I can't get a hold of the data while you're on the phone I'll call you right back."

It seemed to take forever for Uncle Tommy to call me back. I was imagining all sorts of horrible scenarios when my phone rang.

"I've dispatched some men to the location."

"I am the Sheriff! You will damn well, tell me where your man is, now!!"I demanded.

"He's at Buckeye and Lawrence, but he's still not answering.

"I'll send some more of my men there and go myself."

"We will find her and whoever took her will pay," threatened Uncle Tommy.

"Don't do anything foolish. I want this guy, so, he can lead me back to Stella-Marie; because Stella-Marie comes first."

"Of course, Stella-Marie comes first. I love that kid you know that."

"We'll talk later; I'm off, Uncle Tommy."

"Be careful. Your bodyguard is still on your tail; but it wouldn't hurt if you wore a flak jacket,"

"I'll wear the one you gave me; it's in my trunk"

"Fine I'm on my way too. I'll met you there. Hold your temper, son we'll find her."

"I hope and pray you are correct."

I hung up quickly and went to my car grabbing my flak jacket, which I put it on under my clothes. The site was about a half an hour from the school. Despite that Uncle Tommy and his men beat me and my men there. They were standing over a man who seemed to be out cold on the ground. Nearby there was a man that fit the description of Carl the kidnapper. He was also dead ,but he wasn't anywhere near six feet he was probably five foot six ,or seven, near Aunt Louise's size.so why had the administrative assistant lied, or as this another man?

"Are they both dead?" I asked noting the blood on each men's chest.

"He's deader than a door nail!" Uncle Tommy answered, "I called the coroner. He should be here soon."

"God damn it. They can't tell us anything. What about my daughter? Where is Stella-Marie?"

"I don't know, Gee. You better hold it together for Stella-Marie's sake. We will find her!" Uncle Tommy said confidently and for a moment, I almost believed him.

"I'm sorry your man is dead. Did he have family?"

"No, he was a loner, but I will see to a funeral for him. He was one of mine."

"I wish we knew who this other man was now." I said as I watched Uncle Tommy take his fingerprints and a picture of his face and send them to me.

"We soon will I've sent them back to the station and to the Summer F. B. I. agents. If he is in the system; we'll find him and even if he isn't because I sent them to one of my guys," Uncle Tommy whispered.

"Thank -you Uncle Tommy."

My phone rang and I answered it immediately, "Sheriff Bullet."

"Gee, it's Penny. She's here. Stella-Marie is here and she's safe. She just walked into the station."

I breathed a sigh of relief, choking back happy tears. Stella-Marie was safe. I needed to see her now!!

~0~

Chapter 14 - Who was Stella-Marie's Savior?

I rushed into the sheriff station shaking

with relief, Stella-Marie was safe. I looked around went straight to my office, where I found Stella-Marie sitting on Dai's lap. Dai had her arms around her while Stella-Marie was crying. Seeing me, she jumped down, and ran into my arms.

"Daddy...The rest was unintelligible, as she spoke through tears.

"We've tried to get some sense out of her but only Oskâ was able to comfort her," Stoney Summer explained.

"Thank-you, Oskâ," I stated petting the guide dog's head

Then realizing that might not be acceptable, considering Oskâ was a service dog, I apologized to Agent Stoney Summer.

"Oskâ does not have her vest on, so, I'll excuse it this time." Stoney commented, smiling.

"She's a nice doggie, daddy. She helps Agent Summer see better so she doesn't bump into things," Stella-Marie said through tears and hiccups.

"Thank -you for explaining that to me, honey."

I pulled Stella-Marie onto my lap and sat on the sofa in my office. After five minutes of hugs and reassurances, Stella-Marie stopped crying, so I decided to ask her questions.

"So, baby doll what happened? The principal said a man claiming to be Uncle Carl collected you. Did he collect you from your classroom?"

"No daddy. I wouldn't have gone with a stranger. You and Aunt Louise said you said strangers are dangerous.

"I was playing it was recess and Helena said she wanted to play toilet tag. I said I didn't know what that was and she got mad at me and said I was stupid. I ran to the far part of the yard, you know where no one was? I didn't think about strangers there, but that man… that bad man, he pulled me through the chain fence."

"But I thought the school said he presented himself in the office why did he cut through the fence?" Dai asked.

I motioned for her to not interrupt.

"How did he come through the fence?"

"I think he cut it. Like in one of those action movies we watched, because it was a big hole. He pulled me through tucking me up under his arm and he was taking me to this van. This white van with a whole bunch of panels on the side at the curb."

"Wow, you have a great attention to detail Stella-Marie, what else can you tell your daddy?" Dai commented.

"What's attention to detail daddy?"

"It's noticing things pumpkin."

"That's easy. Do we want to tell her more, daddy?

"More about what in particular, honey?" I asked.

"About my mommy! I heard Uncle Andrew say she was bad; that she tried to hurt MY DADDY AND WENT TO JAIL!!" yelled Stella-Marie jumping up suddenly and stamping her foot.

"You heard that?" I gasped.

"I'm not lying!! heard Uncle Andrew say it as I came in the station door. Is my mommy bad? Did mommy send that bad man to grab me?"

"Mommy made a mistake and trusted someone who was naughty. Do you remember that boy who you told me about in your class last year, the one who wanted you not to tell the teacher, when he hurt your friend?"

"Yes, Caleb was mean, but I told the teacher, anyway, because it was the right thing to do."

"Your mommy turned to someone who was naughty, someone who wanted to hurt me, because she was scared. She even helped them a little, but then she was sorry," I explained, wishing she still didn't know.

"She hurt you?"

"Yes, she hurt me, but you know when you do something wrong you have to be punished."

"I know daddy."

"They punished her and she served her punishment and is out of jail now, but she didn't call me, so Uncle Andrew is wondering if the naughty man she was helping before forced her to help him, again,"

"Is she okay, daddy? He's not hurting her, is he?"

"I don't know, but daddy will try to make her safe."

"Love you daddy, Can I tell Dai the secret?

"I love you too and we can tell Dai your secret if you want, but remember; some people don't understand, or like that ability."

"Ability? Stella-Marie has eidetic memory?" Dai guessed.

"I see things and remember them, right, daddy? Is that eidetic memory?"

"That is darling. Not tell me, what did this man look like?" I asked.

"He had dark brown hair and eyes that were black and small like he liked to squint a lot. He was a little shorter, than Aunt Louise though I think he had something in his shoes to appear taller."

"Hmm, so it was the man …" Dai commented ,but cut her sentence off ,when I put my fingers to my lips, because I didn't want Stella-Marie to know people were dead. At least not yet.

"His pants were black jeans and he had on a black hoodie. On the hoodie was a picture of a red A, with a swirly white kind of snow through it. I think it was a fan team shirt," Stella-Marie continued, scrunching up her eyes to remember everything."

"Wow, good work, honey. Now did he say anything to you?"

"He tried to convince me he was my uncle, that you had an Uncle Carl, but I knew you didn't. You told me your uncles' names and I've met them all, but not him! I mean I even met your brother, Blaze last night; now he's an uncle, but not this guy."

"What did his voice sound like?"

"It was deep, but he had an English accent. like one of those shows you watch. You know that murder cop show, with the British people …that's so boring. The cop's name is Barnaby."

"Midsomer Murders with Barnaby... the show you're not suppose to see because you're supposed to be in bed asleep?"

"I was thirsty. I guess I was fibbing, it's not boring."

"Then what happened?" Dai asked.

"He got a mad look on his face and picked me up like I was potatoes and put me under his arm and took me through the fence, towards a van. I fought back and managed to bite his side, he swatted me and I bit his arm and he dropped me. Then a man came out of nowhere and started fighting him. It was like John Claude Van Damm the way he fought, you know like from one of his movies. Except we don't like him anymore; he's too political, right?"

"That's right. What did the man that fought him look like?" I demanded to know.

"I think I saw him before with Uncle Tommy. He was older than a high school

kid, maybe a dad age? He had blonde hair
and a lot of muscles. He was wearing a
black tee-shirt and he took the bad guy down
to the ground and said ,"Run kid." That Carl
guy shot him. I saw the gun and heard the
noise. I thought guns when they used them
went rat-a-tat-tat, but it was boom-boom-
boom. It was so loud and scary, my legs felt
like they were made of cement, but I yelled
at myself and said, "RUN!!" I was afraid the
kidnapping guy would grab me again, or
shoot me, or both. Is the good guy, okay,
daddy? He was trying to help me."

"He helped you baby. He was a good man.
He died, but so did the bad man," I admitted.
"I'm glad you listened."

"Oh, daddy, that poor man. Oh daddy, he
saved me daddy. I got him killed he saved
me," Stella-Marie cried big tears streaming
down her face.

After a few minutes she stopped crying and I
told her, "It's not your fault and he was a
very good man. We will find a way to honor
him, but for now we need to know how you
got to the station, so daddy can make sure
this never happens again. The station is
miles away from where this happened, tell
me please how did you get here?"

"I thought that bad man would kill me. I'm glad the bad man's dead. Is that bad? I'm a bad girl "Stella-Marie started heaving and crying loudly again.

"Honey, it's okay to think that way he scared you. You're not bad."

"Are you sure daddy?" Stella-Marie asked wiping her tears with her sleeve "We will get someone to talk to you about this and make you understand your feelings, but for now can you tell me what else happened?"

"I ran as fast as I could, and ran right into this other man. I was shaking. I thought it was someone else who would hurt me."

"Did he hurt you?"

"No, daddy, he was kind of nice, but I remembered what you said not to trust strangers. The man must have known that, because he pulled out his wallet and said, "I promise, it's safe, honey. You can get into my car and I'll take you to your daddy the sheriff. See here's my licence and here's a picture of a child. I love this child and someone tried to grab him and hurt him and your daddy saved him."

"He showing me a picture of some teenage boy, with brown hair and eyes. He said the boy's name, but I don't remember. That's odd, I always remember. He then said, "I just want you safe. I will take you to your daddy, he's probably at the Sheriff station. Come on I can have you there in a half-an - hour."

"He drove to Driftwood and then parked his car up there and walked me almost here, but he stopped at the building at the corner and pointed to the sheriff building and said, "There, that's where your daddy works. I have to go, but you're safe now, run a long to daddy."

"Did the man say who he was? What did he look like?"

"He had dark hair and was a little shorter than you daddy. he spoke with a Spanish accent, though," Stella-Marie said thinking, "He was really nice, daddy. He didn't hurt me."

"Who the hell could that be? "Dai asked, "A good Samaritan? Whose kid did you help?"

"I'm just glad you're safe Stella-Marie."

"I'm mad at Helena; it's all her fault!!"

"Helena wasn't very nice, but she is your friend. She didn't know that someone was trying to kidnap you."

"Did you daddy?"

"No," I lied.

"Daddy you shouldn't fib. Uncle Andrew was worried about mommy, so, you knew that bad man was out there!" Stella-Marie cried her face twisting up in anger.

"I love you Stella-Marie I would never knowingly put you in danger."

"I'm not stupid, even if I am six. Does mommy really not love me?"

"Your mommy loves you. I think the bad man thought if he took you, he would hurt me ,and make your mommy happy. But I think it would have made her mad, because she knows you want to stay with your daddy."

"Who is this man, daddy? I gotta know What if I see him and he tries to grab me again?"

"That will never happen again. but the man who we suspect was behind this was my former police boss, Derek Chittwood," I answered truthfully and then finding a picture I forgot I had on my phone, I showed her, her mother with Derek."

"He looks like he has shifty eyes," Stella-Marie commented

"Where did you hear that?" Dai asked.

"From Aunt Louise she said the butcher in Detroit had shifty eyes when he tried to cheat her," Stella-Marie answered. "But I don't understand, why is this Mr. Chittwood not in jail?"

"They let Derek Chittwood out for good behaviour and the same for your mother."

"That's not justice ; if he tried to hurt you daddy and tricked mommy, that man should still be in jail."

"I agree, but sometimes justice doesn't work that way."

"Oh yes, like that movie we watched where the guy was a cop and they were trying to hurt him and they almost got away with it all."

"That's right baby we will win."

"I still don't understand, why did that man grab me?"

"Derek wants you, so, your mother will stay with him."

"Oh, he's silly!! She doesn't love him. She still loves you, and me."

"If you see your mother, don't go with her. Do you understand me, Stella-Marie? You run the other way to the nearest safe adult. I will try to let you see her, but only under supervision, when we find her."

"I don't want to see mommy. She's foolish like Elsa in my Frozen movie, wanting to marry some guy she just met. I don't trust mommy at all. She needs someone to talk to her and make her see she's seeing him all wrong."

"You sound like your daddy, "Dai commented.

"That's because I am a Bullet and we are strong and see all, right daddy? Don't worry it won't be me that talks to her."

"That's right my little clone."

"I'm not a clone, but I am a proud Bullet. My head hurts and oops, I'm bleeding,"

Stella-Marie said touching her head and then showing blood on her hand.

"I'm an idiot I should have took you to a doctor right away. Did he hit you with his hand?"

"That man who called himself, Uncle Carl, hit me with a piece of the fence, before I bit him."

"Son of a bitch, I wish he was alive so; I could kill him again." I cried losing my temper.

"Do you want me to take her to the doctor?" Dai asked.

"No," I said coldly, "I'll take her."

"I'll take her, Gee. You need to find out who is behind this," Aunt Louise cried, entering the office.

"Aunt Louise did you hear what happened? A bad man took me, but he's dead! Uncle Tommy's friend saved me."

Aunt Louise looked shocked ,but then she composed herself, saying, "Is that right? "You've been through a lot. Dai's sister called me," Aunt Louise looked reproachfully at me and I mouthed sorry.

"We need a doctor to check your head and your daddy has to find the bad person behind this." Aunt Louise continued.

"I want daddy. He's the only one that can protect me from that man Chittwood."

"She knows his last name?"

I nodded.

"What if your Uncle Gordon looks after you with Aunt Louise?" asked a voice, I recognized walking into my office.

"Uncle Gordon, when did you get here?"

"Uncle Tommy called me and I flew here in a helicopter, as fast as I could. I'm here for at least a month on vacation, pet."

"Stella-Marie will still have to home school every day," Aunt Louise commented.

"At least I won't go back to school right away, with the nasty Helena, this really is all her fault."

"It's not Helena's fault, sweetie, even if she did do something that annoyed you," admonished Aunt Louise.

"I don't forgive her."

"When you're not doing schoolwork, we will play some board games and watch some great movies," promised Gordon, First, however, I will escort you and Aunt Louise to the doctor, so, they can check out your head."

"Is that okay, daddy?" asked Stella-Marie,

"Yes, I've trusted Uncle Gordon with my life and he's never failed me. Thank-you for coming, Gordon."

"I'm always here for you brother. Now let's go Stella-Marie If your daddy can be parted from you, we are off to see the wizard."

"What wizard?" asked Stella-Marie

"A wizard of medicine of course."

"Who?"

'Whichever doctor is at the emergency room."

"You're funny Uncle Gordon."

"That's me, funny man extraordinaire."

I watched them leave feeling a little part of me still terrified, I then went into to my office and locking the door.

I sat down in my chair and began to sob. What the heck was wrong with me Stella-Marie was safe I needed to pull my self together and act like an adult sheriff. So, my arch nemesis, Chittwood had tried to pull off kidnapping my daughter ;but the keyword, was tried. Putting on my game face I went to find Derek and Gina, but I also wanted to know who the good Samaritan was who helped my daughter.

Half-an hour later, I got a call that they wanted to keep Stella-Marie overnight as a precaution, but Aunt Anne promised she'd watch over her tonight, so, that she could go home with Gordon and my Aunt Anne who was a doctor She'd be safe in her own home.

~0~

Afew hours later the phone rang.

"Gee. I'm sending you a text with a picture of the note that Stella-Marie had in her pocket."

"What are you talking about?"

"Stella-Marie woke up and said she forgot to tell us about the note in her pocket from the man who rescue her."

I looked at the texted picture as it came across my phone, there was two pages of notes. I began to read...

Hola Sheriff Bullet

*W*ondering *who it is that saved your*

daughter, from the clutches of that hired henchman? Woah, I sound like a Bond villain, funny thing is I almost like that.

The fact is even though I didn't want to acknowledge it, I owed you a debt which with this act is now paid. I saw an injustice/ crime happening and I stopped it. Why? You ask. Because as I said you did a service for me; you showed me that my bio- brother was not who I thought he was and you looked after my nephew, Frankie. The dear boy was mistreated by that rat bastard has paid for his misdeeds, but Frankie who had never seen any kindness was shown love and kindness from you. You have continued to look after him and make sure he was safe. The boy is doing well and will succeed in his lifetime, as he completes his studies.

I value family above all else and appreciate the time and energy that took, so when someone threatened our family, Stella-Marie(yes, I called her 'our' family, for I plan on marrying her mother. Gina.)

I know Gina did us both wrong, but she has had a lot of growth in the past year. Plus, I know you will congratulate us, Gina is pregnant with my child. I have forgiven Gina, for her transgressions and realize that Chittwood had bewitched and coerced her. Or maybe, he's just taken her, either way he will not have my woman and my child. Chittwood has wronged both of us, so I trust you won't get in my way, as I get my revenge, or should I say 'our' revenge on that bastard, who dared to grab Stella-Marie and scare the poor child.

Don't worry about custody though, I don't plan on taking Stella-Marie, or raising her. Gina and I need time alone and time to raise our own children. Gina however may want to visit on her own, from time to time. That said don't come after us, or I will break this truce and retaliate.

*Keep our daughter safe, don't have your
head so far up your ass that you are left
with your pants down again!!*

*Gordon Chin, although, not my favorite
person is a good choice to keep Stella-
Marie safe. That man is a bulldog. I trust
you will contact Chin, so he too can stay
safe from Derek Chittwood, as I can assure
you, he is on the hit list of Chittwood's.*

Your Frenemy

Luis Cervantes

"Did you read the letter. Gunner?"

"I'm flabbergasted. It was Cerventes who
saved Stella-Marie and he's still fixated on
Gina?"

"The only good thing is that he doesn't want
to fixate on your daughter ,because he has
his own child to worry about."

"Maybe, but he called Stella-Marie, our
daughter. "

"When do you think they got back
together?" Gordon asked.

"I don't know, but I hope he isn't taking advantage of Gina."

"Gunner, you still see Gina as an innocent. The woman tried to kill you. It wasn't all Chittwood's idea to do so. In fact, in the attempted murder trial ,the prosecution tried to prove that it was all Gina's idea."

"They couldn't prove that, because it was all Chittwood's idea."

"Believe what you want to believe; but beware that woman. The F. B. I .informed me yesterday, that Gina was spotted with Chittwood hugging and kissing him."

'Then why didn't they arrest both of them?"

"Chittwood spotted the tail and managed to get them away."

"Cervantes is claiming she's pregnant with his child. She was in prison and now she's with Derek; how does he think that's possible?"

"She had conjugal visits with Cervantes. Apparently, Cervantes pulled some strings to get her out early and was there to pick her up under an assumed name; but she's all ready gone with Chittwood."

"How do you know all this?"

"My contacts have been keeping an eye on Gina so, I knew she might get out early; but she got out even earlier then I was told."

"You didn't tell me."

"I was going to tell you she was out but…"

"What will we do about Chittwood and now with Cervantes back in the mix."

"I'll help anyway I can Gunner ,but I can tell you two of the best F. B. I people are all ready working with you. The Summers are exceptional."

"Yes, I've seen that all ready but won't they be leaving soon."

"Okay, see you in ten minutes, Gordon, and you can explain this to me," I replied curious to know more.

"I can explain over the phone there's a lot to tell; but you are needed there for some of today's paperwork and delegations before heading home."

"You know me well I do have a bunch of things to finish first."

Chapter 15 – On the Case

"**S**o, Cervantes was that guy, who brought Stella-Marie here to Driftwood, then why didn't he take her directly to the station?" Gordon asked me over the phone.

"I really don't know Gordon; but I will find out. That letter was a little odd to say the least."

"If you need any help, I'm sure, I know some guys who could help out."

"Thank -you Gordon, but I thank God, you are watching over my family, because I could never have walked away and get back on the case at work to find Chittwood, which would have seriously impeded my ability to find him. If that bastard thinks he can just send in goons to grab my kid he can think again. Even if we are still working on

the train derailment with the other
organizations I know how to delegate in my
own department and I'll get both solved,
don't worry."

"There's something I didn't tell you.
Something you need to know."

"Quit being so cryptic and let me know the
skinny."

"The train bomb, that was found, they are
pretty sure it went off early. The train would
have gone right by the house I was renting;
but as I said it detonated early. The ATF and
the F. B. I. are starting to wonder if..."

"Are you saying they think someone was
targeting you, Gordon?"

"Yes, but no one knows I'm here you and
Stella-Marie aren't in danger from me. It's
just I thought you should know and no one
is telling you."

"Why didn't either of the Summers tell
me?"

"I'm not sure they know the higher ups are keeping it on a need-to-know basis."

"Son of a …"

"They said I could go to a safe house. I was about to be guarded there; until they solved this. I bought tickets to Las Vegas and a couple of other places, then I borrowed a friend's car and drove here, knowing you'd let me help investigate, Of course, then I found that Stella-Marie had been kidnapped, so I came straight here. Don't worry, though I would never put your family in more jeopardy."

"I'm worried more about you."

"Your Uncle Tommy has guards everywhere and frankly; I'm armed to the teeth; they won't get near your Aunt Louise, or Stella-Marie."

"Just keep yourself and my family safe. I'll send you the investigation notes to look after., but don't go anywhere."

"We won't. Just find that bastard Chittwood and Gina."

"Gina's not behind this," I protested.

"Gunner quit giving her the benefit of the doubt, she isn't a good person and she went willingly with Chittwood."

"You aren't talking about my mom, are you?" Stella-Marie shouted in the background.

"No of course not, I'm talking about a criminal," Gordon lied, coming back on the cell phone he said, "I'll try to find some information from my contacts (on the secure line your Uncle Tommy installed.)"

"If Stella-Marie remembers anything else (without prompting) please let me know."

"Will do," I replied hanging up my cellphone.

I should get back to work. I looked over some reports and the notes which Gordon that suggested Chittwood was in New Mexico, but the description was wrong; the height and eye color was wrong. In the notes Gordon had sent (and the actual notes sent to him from his superiors) they'd spotted them in Las Vegas, a month ago, but apparently, they hadn't been seen since. I looked over the paperwork on the train derailment. The train went by an old line that passed near the F. B. I. headquarters, and Gordon's rental home. What the heck had they planned the bomb to go off at Gordon's home, or the F. B. I. or was this all just a coincidence? Not my investigation the F. B. I. asserted in the paperwork and yet the train had contaminated my town so, the F. B. I. was wrong it was my business. Besides if Derek Chittwood was after Gordon that was because of me. Derek blamed Gordon for his testimony which sent him to jail for his attempted murder of me. The F. B. I. could stop flexing their might, I wasn't going away anytime soon.

~0~

Chapter 16 - The Worst Possible Outcome

It was eight a. m now .I had worked all

night. I probably should be headed home for a few hours catnap; but I had some campaign business to take care of too.

The election was a month a way, with little time to campaign; but surely the populace would appreciate how hard I was working? No definitely not, I thought checking the polls which showed the republican Dick Richards pulling ahead of me in the sheriff's race. My cousin, Kathleen had been making strides in getting paperwork taken care of with the federal government. She and Kasper were enjoying living in Uncle Tommy's other guest house as well. They looked happy when she had dinner with us every few days, but I knew they'd soon be moving back to Denver, when we got this all settled.

Damn, I should be making speeches about law and order. I didn't want to lose my job. I called my campaign manager, Amy Pérez.

"Amy?"

"You've seen the latest polls?"

"I've seen the polls how is Dick beating me?"

"He's making speeches and claiming all the crime started after you arrived."

"There were dirty cops before I arrived, that's why they were killed the day before I arrived."

"Yes, and you may need to tell them in a different way that that's what happened."

"He's also throwing some shade about your late wife. Sorry, about that"

"What is he saying?"

"That your wife was involved in the fentanyl and you used your might to get her off and only married her to save her from jail."

"How dare he?"

"He's a slimeball. I've sent cease and desist orders from a lawyer but the damage may all ready be done the populace is conditioned to believe a lie ,when you tell it enough."

"Am I going to lose the election?"

"I'm not sure, Gee, but you better have a back-up plan just in case. We seem to be one of the few pockets of Colorado that are turning red. Of course, one of the main Trump sycophants is from Colorado so, who knows what will happen election day."

"I hate politics. I wish it could just be an appointment."

"That's not how it works and you knew that when you took the job, Sheriff Bullet."

"Maybe, but I can't believe the people may vote for Dick Richards. How can you trust a guy with that name?"

"He sounds good. He has worked in a big city."

"Where as I understand he wasn't promoted because he's difficult to work with which is why I refused to hire him."

"You think this is all petty revenge?"

"Maybe..."

"We have some time to defeat him. Now, you have a speech tonight, don't be late it's a townhall meeting at 7 p.m." It could be the difference between them believing Dick's lies or believing in you."

"I'll be there," I promised, "I'm going home in a few moments to get some sleep.

"You'd better be, the people need to hear why they should vote for you next week. I'll text your speech in a few minutes. Just memorize it okay?" Amy Pérez insisted and I agreed.

I then left my office and got into my car to drive home. Arriving at the ranch, everything looked fine at first ,but when I got to the checkpoint ;the guards did not come out and demand identification. Had Uncle Tommy called them off. No, he wouldn't do that without notifying me. Had someone broke in?

I went further, finding the second gate open, and down further the bodies of the two guards.

Their bodies were riddled with holes from head to toe, with what appeared to be automatic bullet fire, yet Uncle Tommy had taken all the precautions. How had this happened? How had they been caught them unaware?

A machine gun had taken them out? What the hell? Did Chittwood want everyone dead?

I crept closer. Alarmed, and now on guard, I called in that I had found the bodies .I advised Andrew of my present situation ,that I was not waiting for back-up. Then I took my flak jacket out of my trunk, along with a rifle and some ammo for my guns while Andrew begged me to wait for him or someone else to arrive.

All I could think was, thank goodness that Aunt Anne was the hospital working and Uncle Tommy was meeting her for breakfast, but what about Aunt Louise, Stella-Marie and Gordon? I had to move in fast and hopefully get in before Derek (at least I assumed it must be Derek) took drastic action and fled with Stella-Marie, and possibly harming those I loved as well.

I mentally prepared hoping that Gordon, Aunt Louise and Stella-Marie were okay and I could still save them. I entered the residence ,no alarm going off .Obviously Chittwood had turned them off. Pivoting quietly on my heels, I went towards the sound of loud voices.

"Derak, dear why do you need to take her? Can't you leave Stella-Marie with me?" Aunt Louise asked.

"Look, I have no qualms with you ,old lady, you always treated me well when I came to Gee's house, but Gina needs her daughter, If I have her daughter she can be at peace and live with me; just like we always planned."

"Where is Gina now?'

"She's off with him; he took her but I can find her and save her."

"Dear ,I know you love Gina but has she run off with that criminal, Cervantes, again?'

"Never you mind about that. I'll save her. I told you he's kidnapped her and she has Stockholm Syndrome, but she'll soon be restored to me. Once I have her daughter, safely with me. she'll want to be by my side."

"Sweetheart ,Gina is fickle. You've seen her in action. She doesn't mean to be, cruel and unkind leaving you behind, but if you have seen her mother and grandmother they flit to other men and then go back to the father of their children, who then forgive them. It's a cycle she's been trained to do."

"I can fix that. I can get rid of the father of her child and then she'll look to me ,as the father of her child."

"Don't you hurt my daddy," I heard Stella - Marie shout.

"I'm your daddy now, and you will obey me, Stella- Marie."

"You're not! I have a daddy!!'Stella-Marie responded, loudly stamping her foot.

'Please let me go to Gordon .Gordon is bleeding out. Gordon could die, and if you kill an F. B. I. agent then they could give you the death penalty."

"Fine, but don't try anything woman. As soon as you've bandaged him, I'm tying you up, again. Then we are leaving in a half- an hour, Don't look at me like that. I will call an ambulance for him, just to show you I'm still a good person, Stella- Marie."

"Thank- you, Derek," Stella-Marie stated sweetly.

"I'll take that for now, but when we meet up with your mother , call me daddy. Understand?"

"Ow that hurt," Stella -Marie yelled and then I heard her yell, "Quit twisting my arm, Daddy Derek."

"Closer ,but you remember little girl, I am in charge."

I wanted to throttle Derek, but I had to act smart and get in there and stop Derek in his tracks while protecting all of them. I entered softly behind Derek, two feet from him. I beckoned Stella-Marie to move away from him and raised my gun

"Drop it Chittwood ,"I yelled.

He fired, and I fired, hitting him squarely in the corner of his right shoulder. At first, I didn't realize he'd hit me, as the arm piercing bullet went through my vest and hit my rib. I tried to stay up right; but soon found myself gasping for air as I plunged to the floor, Through the slits of my eyes I saw Stella-Marie pick up my gun. just as I also heard someone come in behind me.

Guns were fired simultaneously and
Chittwood went down, three bullet holes in
his chest ,a direct hit to his heart. Before I
passed out entirely, I knew he was dead ,but
who had killed him? I prayed God it wasn't
my Stella--Marie.

~0~

Chapter 17 - Confusion Reigns

I awakened from a deep REM sleep to finding tubes in my chest, nose and throat. Glancing around I couldn't quite figure out where I was and what I was doing here. Wherever here was. I couldn't keep my eyes open or even think. I closed my eyes and went back to slumberland to the sound of whooshing and loud beeping machines.

I awoke, sometime later, and saw Aunt Louise sitting there.

"Am I late for school?" tried to ask her, but the words were intelligible. I couldn't quite figure out where I was, or why.

I struggled trying to pullout the tubes, when a nurse came in and injected something into the tube in my hand. I went back to sleep awaking again later and Blaze was sitting there and the tube that was in my throat, I assume breathing for me was gone ,replaced by a tube in my nose.

"Is he dead?' I asked Blaze.

"Stella-Marie gave the gun to you and we both fired at the same time. My bullets and yours striking simultaneously and killing Chittwood instantly."

"Thank -you for arriving at he right time, Blaze," I commented realizing what he was really saying, Stella-Marie's bullet had helped kill Chittwood and he told everyone it was me, to protect his niece.

"Nothing any law enforcement, or brother would have done," Blaze answered, "Don't worry I gave an official statement that we killed Chittwood not anyone else. I'm sure Andrew will be sent to get your official statement. I was never here at least, not yet for you statement so no collusion,"

Is Stella-Marie, okay?"

"Aunt Louise is taking Stella- Marie to a child psychologist , Dr. Armand, who says she's doing well but she be better when you wake up. " Stella -Marie's been here several times sneaking into to see if you are still breathing and whether you are awake. She'll be pleased to see you."

"They allowed her to come in? to ICU?"

Blaze rolled his eyes. "This is your daughter ;there's really no stopping her."

"Is Gordon alive?"

A curtain in the next bed was drawn back and Gordon looked over at me grinning.

"Can't get rid of us that easy, can they?" Gordon commented.

"I'm so glad you're alive I thought you were dying."

"Your Aunt Louise kept both of us alive until the ambulances took us away"

"What was Chittwood's plan and who helped him with the train? He couldn't have done all that himself.!" I demanded.

"Andrew is working on that," Blaze answered ,"Also with the help of myself and the F. B. I agents Summer."

"Have they got any leads yet?"

"I suspect that the F. B. I may be keeping some of the evidence close to the chest.

They are not sharing as much , at least that
what Andrew suspects and any information
is coming from the higher ups ;but good
news the train engineer will live (he has
along recovery period ahead of him)the bad
he has no memory of the accident and likely
never will."

'Can you used your connections, Gordon
and find out more about the case?"

"I've been trying from my bed, but they've
clamped down on a lot of my sources. It's
like they think I'm in the ICU suffering from
a bullet wound," Gordon joked, "I gave my
official statement too but I was unconscious
when Chittwood was shot. Your cousin,
Kathleen has been helpful though. She has
fed me some information."

"Or they think both of you ,are too close, to
the case," Blaze answered.

"Andrew is not too close," I protested.

"Luna is dating Andrew, you know that."

"I thought they broke up."

"No, they are back together, in fact ,they are
getting married. They got engaged

yesterday, so the F.B.I. probably think he's way to close, because she's Gina's sister."

"Andrew is a true-blue cop, through and through. The guy bleeds truth and justice. As for Luna she'd never help Gina commit a crime. What the heck is wrong with their thinking? As much as I like Luna; I can see why they'd question her; but Andrew would never participate in anything like that how dare they question his integrity?"

"Yes, Dick Richards is smearing you and Andrew with this."

"The election is a month a way, we've got time. To straighten out the voters," I answered.

"You've been here almost a month ,Gee. The election is tomorrow. You might get some sympathy votes ,but it is looking bad. Dick hates Andrew, and I so we will be the first to go."

"I guess I'm looking for a new job, but you have to smuggle me out, so I can at least vote."

"I'll try, but first I'll have to get by the dragon."

"Dragon?"

"There she is," he whispered, as a nurse came in and conversation was stopped.

"Are you agitating my patients, sir?" she asked.

"No ma'am, "Blaze said contritely.

"Your ten minutes is up with your brother, and my patients need their rest, Besides the doctor will be here shortly."

"Yes, ma'am," Blaze answered.

"I'll be back later," Blaze said winking at me.

Andrew came in and I signed my official statement about Chittwood's death. This would soon be completely over at least with the paperwork my daughter was another story, I hoped she was all right. I need to see her.

Blaze then left as the doctor entered and told me how lucky I was to be alive .He then told me I needed to take it easy, that although I wasn't on the critical list anymore, I could still harm my health if I didn't rest. I didn't care about that nonsense, if Blaze could

smuggle me out in a wheelchair I was voting
and so, was Blaze, hopefully for me.

After the doctor left, I fell asleep again.
Frankly, I think with a little help from
something they put in my IV. Blaze was
back when I awoke trying to move me into a
wheelchair with an oxygen tank and an IV
poll. He cast his eyes into the corridor then
smuggled me out the door and into the
elevator. I was still dressed in a hospital
gown with a blanket over my lap but since
the poll station was next to the hospital I
didn't have far to go.

Blaze put me in the elevator and then
smuggled me out a back door of the hospital
and then to the polling station.

He had my identification and all the other
things I needed to vote so I was set.

When I entered the long line people cleared
the line for me urging me to go ahead of
them until I found myself at the start of the
line. Blaze pushed ,me in and they allowed
him to push me over to a booth, where I
voted. I'd done all I could it was in the
voter's hands now. Tomorrow I would know
if I still had a job ;but Blaze knew I needed

to get back to my bed as I guess had turned
pale ,as I felt faint.

Blaze got me back to the bed, but not
without the dragon and the doctor
admonishing him, as I floated off to oblivion
once more.

~0~

Chapter 18 – Election Woes

Days later, I awoke in a regular hospital bed, the elections were long over. Andrew was there and revealed to me ,that I had lost as expected to Dick Richards. Even saying his name made me feel ridiculous. How could the people have betrayed themselves like this? I know six people had been killed in the initial derailment of the train and the engineer would suffer his entire life with his injuries, even though he survived. I grieved for those people and their families; but we had prevented the town from having more deaths ,shouldn't that have counted?

The only good news from the election, if you could call it good news, was Andrew telling me that Uncle Tommy was the new mayor. Uncle Tommy's first official duty had been keeping that corporation

Metaphysical Spas Inc (which Jared Brentwood had been bought in to the election to advocate for them expropriate any land in Driftwood they needed.) from expropriating Uncle Tommy's own property and basically forbidding Metaphysical Spas Inc from buying property in Driftwood County. How he had got that worded, so, accurately, and effectively, was stupefying to Metaphysical Spas Inc, but not surprising to me.

Andrew told me that Uncle Tommy had told him privately, Uncle Tommy had threats to his person , which could not be traced conclusively to them. Uncle Tommy was mad, he knew the had threats and where they were from. So, he had hired the best lawyer minds in the country to draft contracts to keep Metaphysical Spas Inc out of Driftwood permanently. Uncle Tommy and his lawyers were trying to trace the owners through the numbered company they were hiding behind ,but so far it had not been possible. Andrew also told me he was working for Dick Richards ,because he needed the work, but that the man was incompetent.

"The man has no empathy, no communication skills, he is vague when issuing assignments and you know others don't work well without instructions. I can operate affectively, but the other cops especially the newbies he's brought in have no skills and can't cope. When Richards does communicate it's with yelling. He's disrespectful, and has poor leadership skills. He openly shows hostility to me and I'm the only one keeping the station actually solving anything."

"Can you list anymore?" I asked.

"I get it !I'm complaining too much, but the guy is impossible. You don't know what is like working with such an arrogant, narcissistic boss."

"Yes, I think I do, but he's dead now."

"I get it Chitwood!! At least Richards hasn't tried to kill me twice. Too soon?"

"Finally getting a sense of humor, Andrew? Seriously though, what about the damage to our town? From the train derailment how can we move forward?"

"Your Uncle Tommy had a fundraiser. He contributed a million dollars of his own money to help clean up the mess. Then he hired this company which is now cleaning it all up. They should be finished by the end of the month." We also sued the train company but we probably won't win."

"Wow, amazing ! I shouldn't be surprised Uncle Tommy always seems to get things done."

"The populace seems to be really happy with their new mayor . They are starting to see Sheriff Richards in a new light though. Ha, ha. Not too many people who meet him like him, now."

"I expected a visit from Agent Dai Summers, but she's nowhere to be seen."

"Yes, sorry boss I mean Gee. She left town with her sister. They are wrapping up their investigation here in Driftwood They've centered on Denver and the tracks where the bomb had been planned to go off. They seem to be looking into all the ties to Chittwood, but so far, they hadn't been able to trace his associates beyond a few minor characters. The scuttle is they are putting the screws to those but they were too scared to reveal anything. I'm sure you'll see your cousin soon though. She's commuting from here to Denver."

"So, Agent Dai Summer is gone, no note nothing?' I asked,

"Here's a note from Agent Summer. She told me it was personal, "Andrew said lifting an eyebrow .

Dai had probably sent a note to me probably to tell me thanks for the memories ,but I wasn't quite ready to read it yet, so I tossed it to one side.

"Deputy Ambercrombie, I told you could stay ten minutes it's been a half- an hour. My patient needs rest. If you stay any longer, you'll soon be disturbing his roommate, Mr. Chum who will be joining him this afternoon."

"Where's Gordon been?" I asked.

"Mr. Chum has been in a private room; but requested to join you when you were moved into this room, He'll be here later this afternoon ,when we are ready for him," the nurse answered.

"I'll go now. nurse. My lunch hour is over anyway, but I'll be back later or you can call me Gee," Andrew replied.

My lunch was delivered soon after. Clear soup, jello and tea. Yum, so appetizing. Never the less I found myself eating it. The sooner I got my strength back, the sooner I would be out of this hospital. I glanced at the letter and put it aside again, only to pick it up a few minutes later. I slit the envelope with my fingertip; my nails having grown longer while I was resting. The nails definitely needed cutting I thought. Enough delaying I thought read the letter.

Gunner

I'm sorry, I can't say goodbye in person. I hope that you'll understand duty calls. Given all that has happened, I've had a lot of time to think about things. I care about you, but I meant it, I want no strings. I fear that maybe this isn't something you can live with, given that you have a young child. So, I'm leaving it all here, maybe some time in the future we will meet to play again, but only if you are still willing to play to my rules .Adieu until we meet again

Dai

I should have expected this ,but somehow, I
hadn't. I told myself I was going to break it
off with her but the truth was I still cared
about her despite her rules. She was correct I
really wasn't the friends with benefits kind
of guy. Sex wasn't just sex ,because my
feelings were always involved, I realized
belatedly. Maybe, I should stay away from
women for awhile. I always seem to get my
heart broken. My sad, feeling sorry for
myself feelings, were interrupted by Uncle
Tommy sneaking in my hospital room .

"Getting better, boy?"

"Yes, I'll be home soon, I hope."

"You know you lost the election and you are
out of a job?"

"I wouldn't put it that way, but yes, Andrew
told me Dick Richards is the sheriff."

"That guy is crooked as the day is long. I
don't trust that man. I don't understand how
he could have won the election."

"Richards won. I'll live with it. What about
you ?I hear you are facing threats again;
you've hired more help though to protect
you .correct?"

"I have a full protection team, and in six weeks when the doctor clears you, I have a job for you if you're willing."

"A pity job?"

"Are you saying he gave me a pity job?" Blaze asked walking in.

"Where did you come from?"

"The hall, I'm Uncle Tommy's bodyguard,"

"Is that what you are offering me?' I asked.

"Blaze is just filling in, until I get new help, I have a plan for you both."

I gave Uncle Tommy a look.

"It's not illegal .I know you boys stick to the straight and narrow."

"Then what is it?'

"Not here the place has ears," Uncle Tommy insisted.

"It's honest work he briefed me, "Blaze promised and then he gestured that he was stepping back into the hall.

"You'll be living at the ranch with me until you are fit boy. I want you safe. Stella-

Marie, and Louise are already there. Don't worry I've beefed up security no one will get in without my say so."

"I'm not lazing around."

"You'll do what the Doctor Anne says. She'll be looking in on you and believe me she's tough. She'll get you back in tip top shape."

"She keeps you in line."

"She's the only one ,I've ever been scared of, "Uncle Tommy admitted.

"Who are you and why are you in my patient's room without permission?" asked an angry nurse coming in.

"Sorry ma'am .I guess you didn't see me this is my nephew, and I've been so worried."

"Why aren't you the mayor?"

"Yes ma'am, I've been very busy running Driftwood and have only got news from others. I had to see my nephew for myself."

"I can appreciate that mayor but my patient is tired I see and I'd like him to rest."

"Of course, ma'am., I'll go now but I'll be back tomorrow ,nephew."

"See you tomorrow, Uncle Tommy," I replied as the nurse smiled, at Uncle Tommy and ushered him out.

I was thinking about how, I was looking forward to be home with my daughter and stubbornly resisted going to sleep; but my body betrayed me and against my will, my eyes closed.

~0~

Chapter 19 - Criminal Enterprise is Moving into Driftwood

I had required sufficiently to work for

Uncle Tommy, as his bodyguard; but he also had Blaze and a number of other people looking into election malfeasance. Uncle Tommy believed that a number of people in Driftwood County and Tear Drop Canyon had their votes disenfranchised. So far, we'd found no real proof, only vague whispers of people complaining they didn't vote for so and so. Cousin Kathleen had hung around with her husband Kasper Kristiansen. She was wanting to live in Driftwood part-time and work in Denver permanently if she could and Uncle Tommy agreed,

Uncle Tommy said that Dick Richards was bought and paid for and he would prove it. He was getting very agitated about, it even though I told him I could survive without being the sheriff of Driftwood, Uncle Tommy simply wasn't listening. He hated injustice and he hated that Dick Richards had stolen my job. He was beginning however, to hint to that in public and that was bad for him and for me; even if we had the proof (and we didn't we didn't want Richards alerted as well as whoever had helped him.) Besides Uncle Tommy was the mayor, they could impeach him. Besides I worried that he would slip into old ways and go too far. I made him promise that he wouldn't, but I still worried.

Stella-Marie was having a few nightmares about what happened when she killed er Blaze killed Chittwood. The child psychologist , Doctor Armand, was helping though and Stella-Marie was back at school with her classmates. Soon she'd be able to come back to school in Driftwood the clean-up I had arranged (and now Dick was taking credit for) was almost done. In fact, most of Driftwood was free from the damage the train had caused.

Uncle Tommy had me working only eight-hour days five days a week so, I could spend more time with her. I almost became happy

., I say almost ,because I loved police work. I wasn't a sheriff . I missed the people I used to work with though Andrew and Penny Ambercrombie were still working at the police station. They'd come to visit me at least once a week, like they were worried about me; but they were good friends and I appreciated them.

The phone interrupted my weekend breakfast. Aunt Louise had spirited Stella-Marie to a shopping spree in Denver and I was to meet them there for diner tonight. We'd stay the night and then tomorrow after church services there we'd have a light lunch and drive back.

"Haven't you left yet ,boy? You'll be late if you don't get a move on," Uncle Tommy said, as if he was in the same room.

"Do you have someone watching me?' I asked.

"Now would I do that?"

"Yes," I answered.

"Okay, so you caught me. Have fun in Denver. Blaze and I will hold down the fort here in Driftwood."

"Just don't cross any lines, that's all I ask,
"I stated.

"I'll behave myself ,as long as Dick doesn't
cross any lines."

"Uncle Tommy if he crosses lines call the F.
B. I. don't act, you understand me?"

"I'll be a good boy. You know that your
Aunt Anne keeps me on a long chain."

I said goodbye and drove to Denver arriving
in plenty of time to have a coffee and wait
for Aunt Louise and Stella-Marie to come
back.

I was waiting in the café with full view of
the front of the hotel when a young man
dressed in a delivery service uniform walked
up to me and handed me a letter then left.

To say I was surprised was an
.understatement. I threw caution to the wind
and opened the envelope.

In it was a letter I read

Bullet

Gina is my wife. There, I got that over with.
So, you know we are family now. Your
Stella-Marie is my step-daughter. I know

however you still have your moral code, so I won't step on your toes and bring any criminal activity where our beloved Stella-Marie lives. I am sorry the people of Driftwood are so foolish and rewarded all your hard work with defeat.

There I have put words of comfort in as Gina asked, don't think this is me being soft. Okay. Maybe a little soft. Yes, that's correct .Gina will have my baby boy soon. Stella-Marie will be a big sister, but she may not see her brother, until she's all grown up and she can make her own decision.

Yes, Gina put that in. She loves her daughter ,but she doesn't want to be arrested and torn from our son.

Gina wants me to inform you (against my wishes) that you are in danger which means that Stella-Marie is in danger as well, which is the only reason I am informing you. Now there is a huge criminal organization moving into Driftwood and the new sheriff is not only turning a blind eye, Richards may be part of the criminal organization. I don't have to tell you to protect our daughter. Yes, I think of Stella-Marie that way; but I won't interfere in any way. Maybe I shall just let my son share my old name .I look forward to our next meeting Bullet. Au revoir mon ami, or should I say, mon ennemi.

Louis

I couldn't believe it he'd written again. he was using French ,was he in France, or maybe Quebec, Canada? Would I ever hear the last of him? Was Gina with him of her own free will, or was she expecting a rescue from me? No. she did seem to love him before. I couldn't turn a blind eye anymore; she loved the bastard. Gina had forgiven him for killing her sister. Who could do that?

Gina was a lost cause but least she cared enough about her daughter to warn us about the criminals who were moving into Driftwood ;even if Luis (or Louis as he was calling himself now) kept it vague.

I really hated this part. I was the sheriff and now I was not! I couldn't get access to the information I needed. There was only one person to turn to. I picked up my phone and called Uncle Tommy informing him of what Luis had told me and he promised to look into it. I had to get my head right there was nothing I could do right now and my daughter was coming into the hotel ,time to put on my smile and have fun, Stella-Marie had seen enough crime maybe I needed to move out of Driftwood? No between her Great-Uncle Tommy, her Uncle Blaze and her Uncle Gordon who was still on leave and staying at the house, we'd all be safe and I'd be damned if I'd let someone take over Driftwood without a fight.

~0~

The End until External Ballistics coming 2027~Excerpt on the next page.

Excerpt from External Ballistics

I had a great night with my little girl.

Last night, Stella-Marie had shown me all her new clothes and some cheap plastic jewellery she'd picked up. She treated the plastic jewellery, as if it was diamonds. I was just glad she was acting so happy. It had been heartbreaking, to see my little girl so unhappy, the last month. Christmas was in three days and she had some parcels she was desperate to hide. I just smiled and allowed her confidences. I actually had her presents all ready ordered and wrapped under the tree, except for what Santa would bring. We would have a good old fashion Christmas, and forget about the criminals until the day after Christmas. I wasn't the sheriff anymore; I could take a break from Uncle Tommy's problems; I told myself and my little girl needed this.

We had spent the last hour in church. I'd thank God for my rescues over the last years , something that was way overdue. We celebrated thinking of the joy of Christmas to come. I was excited, I would be home for an entire Christmas day with my little girl. It was when we exited the church and I turned my phone on, that I noticed all the missed calls on my phone. Most from a number I didn't recognize and three from Andrew. I

"I have to make some calls I'll meet you at the plaza for lunch ," I told Stella-Marie and Aunt Louise.

I was just about to redial Andrew when my phone rang again.

"Gunner?" the voice on the other end of the phone cried.

"Aunt Anne?" I asked recognizing the voice.

"Thank God ,you finally answered. I'm at my wits end and they won't let me see him."

"What's happened?" I demanded, worried because I'd never heard her panic, it just didn't seem in her nature.

"They say he's dead, but I don't understand."

"Who is dead? Is Uncle Tommy dead?'

"No, Sheriff Dick Richards is dead. Tommy is in the hospital; he's been shot. He might die and they won't let me see him. They say Tom killed Richards, but I know he wouldn't, he wouldn't break his promise to me. Besides he had no reason to kill the bastard."

"Who won't let you see him?"

"That deputy Richards promoted. His name is Alan something…I think, but I have heard them also call him Richard. I think Richards found it confusing too and that's why some call him Alan. He has taken over as Sheriff, because Richards is dead. If you can believe it, he fired Andrew and Penny at the hospital when they showed up for me."

"Are you talking about Richard Alan Pick?"

"Of course, that's' the name. He has three names like Lee Harvey. I wouldn't trust that so-called acting sheriff.

"I can't believe they think Uncle Tommy killed anyone. If Uncle Tommy killed someone he wouldn't be caught at the scene."

"I know right! They have the wrong man. Pick won't listen; he says I'm biased and treats me like a little woman. He has no idea that I am still an acting F. B. I agent and I'm not telling him , not until I can oust the jerk. I'm also kind of worried about that other guy Pick has appointed, his new deputy Petrov Volkov or Pete Volk as he has shorten his name to. I think Tommy was on to something. He told me cryptically he believed there were criminals working at the sheriff's office. I can't find any background on these people other than the one they've planted. Volk and Pick are not their real names and what better way to take over the police force than to infiltrate it and get rid of anyone who actually cares about justice?"

"Maybe that's true Aunt Anne, but Uncle Tommy also believed Dick Richards was crooked and I trust in that belief. Could he have been crooked enough for Uncle Tommy to shoot him? No, I won't believe it. The only way it could have happened that way is if Richards shot Uncle Tommy first. Frankly, I think it was just a wrong place, wrong time, for Uncle Tommy and they just went with it to get rid of two birds with one stone. Don't you worry Aunt Anne I'm going to collect Stella-Marie and Aunt

Louise and will be home in a couple of hours, unless I get a ticket for speeding. I'll get to the bottom of this and I will also make them let you see Uncle Tommy. It will be okay we have pretty strong blood and Uncle Tommy will fight this, or my name isn't Gunner Bullet."

"Thank- you Gunner, Tommy said he could always count on you in an emergency, Drive carefully see you soon."

"See you soon, Aunt Anne. Remember family takes care of family and we love you."

"Love you ,too, Gunner dear."

I hung up and practiced what I'd say to Stella-Marie that wouldn't scare her, because she adored Uncle Tommy. I was going to make whoever had done this pay because they had shot and framed my uncle, and now they were wrecking my little girl's Christmas. The bodyguard could drive them home to Driftwood this afternoon, so, they'd be safe. As for Acting Sheriff Pick, I had news for him. according to the rules of our county since I was runner-up, I had the right to take over as sheriff until a new election was called and I was about to exercise my rights so he'd better stay the hell out of my way.

The phone rang again seconds later.

"Gunner?"

"Something else Aunt Anne?"

"Your uncles , James, Benjamin, and Alfred Bullet have arrived. Did know they were coming for Christmas?"

"No, this day just keeps getting better and better.

"I'm on my way. I hate to ask but can you keep them busy until I can get aunt Louise to them?"

"These guys are like an overdose of testosterone but your cousin Kathleen seems to be taking all the heat from them."

"Did they find out about her husband, Kasper Kristiansen?"

"Yes, , and her father and the other two were mad, that she didn't invite them to the wedding. They felt they should be able to check him out but I think they are coming around."

"I'll be there soon. Don't worry I'm their favorite punching bag they'll lay off Kathleen and Kasper, completely, once I get there."

"See you so, Gunner. Remember you can't choose your relatives; you can choose who you associate with."

This ought to be a riotous Christmas to remember ,I thought. And not the Christmas I'd planned.

~0~

If you enjoyed this excerpt read more of External Ballistics available in late 2027.Please also check out any of my many other titles listed on page 387, available at your favorite realtor.

Sincerely S. G. Lee

~*0*~

Excerpt from Jack be Nimble

Sucker

It all started Monday morning and boy, I hated Monday mornings. As I climbed the steps to my tiny office, I could feel the waves of heat; already seeping through my cheap suit. It was hot enough to fry an egg out there and it was only eight a.m. The door was stiff in the heat and I noted that someone had tried to break in. There were scratches by the door. Everything looked in its place. The cabinet with my files was still locked as was my desk, obviously an attempt to break in, but not a success on their behalf. My half- empty bottle of cheap hooch was still there.

I threw my hat up on the coat rack in the
corner and peeled off my suit coat jacket
hoping that my window fan would kick in
soon. Then I took the bag, I carried with my
breakfast, over to the coffee cup on the
shelf. I cracked the two eggs into it and then
poured orange juice over them. Oops, almost
forgot the chaser a little Tabasco sauce.
Good for what ailed me, as my head ached
from the cocktails, I'd imbibed last night. I
then sat in my desk chair, blessing the fact
that I had been gifted by a client with a chair
which had swivel wheels. I swiveled for a
bit, then turned and faced my door; wishing
for a client to breeze in to end my boredom.

I read my etched name, Jack Daniel Forbes
private investigator, on the door for the
fifteenth time. I twirled in my chair once
again, to look at it and found a woman
standing there. And not just any woman, this
woman was a knock-out.

She had blonde hair in fashionable chignon.
A real looker ,with her bright blue eyes and
come-hither smile, and gams that went on
and on. Her skirt was split up to the knee.
She had the look of that movie star... you
know the one ,I mean. Carol Lombard now,

she was classy, not like that Mae West who you couldn't bring home to your mother. Except the dame wasn't smiling, but grimacing, as if to keep from crying. As she pulled out a tear-stained handkerchief and walked over closer to me; I could see her eyes were red and puffy as well.

"Are you Mr. Forbes?" she asked her voice musical even when trembling.

"Yah, I'm Jack Daniel Forbes like the sign says," I answered, intrigued by whatever she wants to tell me.

"Can I trust you?" she asked.

"I'm very trustworthy ma'am, unless you've committed a crime, there are no worries on that score," I reassured her.

"I have to trust someone. I'm going out of my mind," she stated hesitating "Maybe if I knew a little bit more about you?"

"Well, you know the skinny on me. My name is Jack Daniel Forbes. I was copper for ten years, until the heat got a little too hot when I turned in some flatfeet, for being on the take. That old blue wall went up and this detective was down for the count, until I opened up my own private investigation office three years ago."

"That's all very interesting, I suppose, but I still don't know that I should trust you. If word should get back...."

"I was named after the whiskey bottle my mother finished the night ,I was conceived. Hey, why did I tell you that? That's a little bit too personal, sorry." I blurted out knowing ,that I was lying ;but hey I couldn't help myself. Didn't I tell you she was a looker? She looked at me, like I had two heads

Surprising myself ,I continued making an effort. I felt that I fumbled a little there, something about this dame made me want to reveal everything about myself, to her. Of course, I did the dance, a little charm and schmooze ,that I was famous for and I felt she'd be putty in my hands. She wasn't. She seemed immune to my charisma or should I say my charms.

I rarely brought up my childhood, even to lie about it. What had I been thinking? I had been a cop for ten years ,and I did turn in a flatfoot on the take break the code of blue. I had escaped my criminal childhood years before that. My real moniker was Giovanni Fabbrizzo Junior, better known as little Johnny or Jack Giovanni in the neighborhood where I grown up and I used to run numbers for my daddy's best friend. Until I had my ears boxed. Wait a minute; forget what I said ,and forget you heard that name, I'm Jack Daniel Forbes now that's my moniker and don't forget it.

"No, I appreciate your candor; I'm not much for banter anyway. I suppose I can reveal things about myself as well. My name is Mrs. Grace-Ellen Parks and someone is trying to kill me," she blurted out and then began sobbing all over the place.

Now am I sucker ,when a woman cries? I can't stand the wallowing. It does something to me. My insides turn to Jell-O and all I want to do was take her in my arms, but she said she was a Mrs., and I respect the bonds of matrimony. So, I just patted her arm saying there, there, and handed her the handkerchief out of my suit coat jacket.

"You are a gentleman, aren't you?" she said glancing at me in surprise and wiping her eyes gently patting them.

"I try ma'am, "I replied thinking she had all
the ear markings of a vulnerable woman
who I could sashay into my bed, when this
had been wrapped up.

"My husband is trying to kill me!" she
stated, in a stage whisper, as if she was
afraid to say it.

"No, you have to be mistaken. He'd have to
be crazy, to get rid of a knock-out of a broad
like you," I replied.

"I am not mistaken. Maybe you weren't the
right man for the job, after all," she
exclaimed rising in a graceful way.

"No wait, Mrs. Grace-Ellen Parks. If your
ball and chain really tried to do away with
you, then you need someone like me to
prevent it."

"I don't know what to do what if I'm
wrong? I wouldn't want it getting back to
my ex-husband," she retorted.

"Ex, but you just said he was your husband."
I protested.

"A slip of the tongue, he divorced me a few
months ago, but my Daddy, Judge Banks got

me alimony. I'm not poor, I can pay your fee," she explained.

"Oh, so that's it, your ex wants to rid himself of you to stop letting out his pockets. We can fix that."

"Do you think that's it?" she asked excited.

"Yes," I replied proudly.

"Come to my house at six p.m. so we can plan some more. Here's the address. Don't be late," she demanded then added with a kiss she blew at me, "Goodbye, Sir Launcelot."

I stewed most of the afternoon wondering what, she expected me to do at six p.m. Am I just the muscle to her? I'm not in the business, just to be a fathead. That's the way a guy gets hurt ,or possibly killed in this job. But the dame needed help as long as he wasn't a trigger man. I was safe. But just to be safe I'd bring my shooter.

At five twenty-five p.m. I went to my desk drawer to get my gun ,a Remington .41 caliber Double Derringer. My only purchase ,when becoming a private detective, this

baby was my pride and joy. I had my throw
away strapped to my ankle calf. It would
certainly defend the dame from her
murderous ex. I turned the key and to my
surprise no gun. Damn someone had gotten
in here after all, and they had my gun. Why
hadn't I noticed its absence earlier? I would
have to report it missing, later to some of my
buddies, ones I still had left ,on the force. I'd
be late if I didn't hurry. Thank goodness, I
had my trusty back-up. It wasn't as nice or
even as accurate in my opinion, but it would
do in a pinch.

I arrived at the address a few minutes before
six p.m. to see the door, a jar. Had he gotten
in ahead of me? I bounded up the stairs to
hear a gunshot. Was I too late? I ran into the
house ,hoping to find her and save her. I
heard yet another gunshot coming, from the
upstairs bedroom. I bounded up the stairs,
opened the door, to find her holding the gun
over a man bloodied on the floor. He had a
huge wound in his chest. he now bled
heavily from. She had shot him straight
through the forehead ,the second time. That
was not a pretty picture, as the blow back
disgusted me, to say the least. She stood
frozen, as if in shock and then the shivering
began. I went to the bedroom next door and

grabbed a blanket, throwing it around her shoulders. Poor woman! She'd defended herself and this was the result; then I noticed my missing gun lying beside his body.

"He tried to kill me. I shot him," she croaked.

"Yah, you're all wet, muffin. You took my shooter and you plugged him. Clearly it was premeditated," I complained, loudly.

"I had to, I was so scared," she answered, tears pooling in her eyes again,

What could a man do? I could only stand those tears so long; I took her in my arms and comforted her, only to have her push me, into the bedroom next door. I let matters get out of hand and the next thing I know the cops break in, guns a blaze to find us in flagrante delicto. She's crying rape, and saying I killed her husband. She's shaking like a leaf and they're buying her every word. I was toast. You look at me and you look at her and who would you believe?

We were both arrested, her sticking to her
story, that I killed her husband and had tried
to rape her. (Yes, he was her husband, not
her ex as she claimed.) She claimed I stalked
her and her husband had spoken severely to
me. Then I had plotted to kill him to have
her.

It seemed I was in a fix. I used my one
phone call to reach out to my buddy on the
force, Pat O'Malley. I hadn't seen Pat in a
few years, but Pat was eager to prove that
Grace-Ellen was a fraud and a murderess.

I was in jail nearly a week, before the key
came to breaking Grace-Ellen's story came
out. I stored the gun in my desk drawer ,but
the bullets? The bullets were stored in my
room under the floorboards. Grace-Ellen had
to buy bullets so she could plug her
husband. Pat O'Malley canvassed many
stores and finally tracked down the gun shop
Grace-Ellen bought the bullets at.

Grace-Ellen screamed and ranted and raved
that it wasn't her, but the guy that sold her
the bullets. It seemed like a she said he said
moment yet again; until the Bruno's wife
stepped up and said that she had seen that
woman Grace-Ellen in their shop.

Grace-Ellen decided to give them the
lowdown; at least her version of the truth.
She still continued to claim she was a
battered wife and she had enough she took
my gun for protection and bought the bullets
only to protect herself. She almost had them
believing it ,but the first guy she tried to hire
to knock off her husband came forward and
put the kibosh on that. She'd promised him
herself and a lot of money; but he was
playing for the other team and he wasn't
interested. Grace-Ellen ranted and raved
about that one and threatened to reveal his
sexuality. She kept calling the man a poof.

He told them her that he didn't care what
she said, he didn't liked, the opposite sex
and people would just have to accept him.
He then confessed that Grace-Ellen had been
plotting all this for a while and I was just the
patsy she picked. Seemed like nice enough
fellow. Maybe people should live and live.
What happens behind closed doors ain't no
business of mine or yours, I'm thinking. Of
course, the man had just saved my hiney and
I was grateful.

When Pat started searching the system from
state to state a minor miracle occurred, Pat
reached the right ears and eyes.

Mrs. Grace-Ellen Parks had done this before
in three different states, each time picking
out a patsy for the fall guy. She was a black
widow, getting rich of the proceeds of each
of her husbands' demise. One of those men
she had conned, had been hung for her
crime; the other two awaited their execution
in the electric chair. The cops who had
convicted the men drove to our town and
when they saw Grace-Ellen they were able
to identify her under several different
names. Turns out the one flatfoot said
Grace-Ellen wasn't even her real name. Her
name was really Eunice Perkins from Arley
Alabama. Seems they wanted her there too.
She'd killed her whole family there and took
every penny they had. As for me, I'm very
grateful to Pat O'Malley for saving my
bacon.

Pat is a gem. She loves being a cop; despite
the fact that they don't respect her. She is
better than most those cops at her precinct,
but they stick her with typing jobs and
traffic patrol. All those jobs that none of
them want to do. Pat wasn't just a police
administrator, I could banter with; she was a
woman and a darn good investigator. She
was the one that tracked down all the
information on that woman. Damn, those

other flatfeet. I hated that they didn't respect her.

I wore Pat down and we started seeing each other quite a bit. What can I say I'm a sucker for tears and when she cried because I was free, I saw Pat in a new light. She didn't even throw my fumble in my face and when I glanced at her, I saw true beauty and grit.

Pat and I began a dance. I'd soirée her around from time to time and sometimes she'd pretend that is what she wanted. Other times she would date a fellow cop. A mistake if I ever saw one ;but you can't tell someone you're the guy for them. I'd wear her down, I vowed.

Summer turned into autumn and I took her to the Harvest dance. We danced the night away and I was convinced ;I had her in the palm of my hand when he walked in... one Sergeant Ray Walters. He told Pat he'd been looking forward to meeting one of his fellow flatfeet. Who pointed Patty out, I don't know; but they didn't do either of us any favors.

I hated Ray Walters from the minute I met
him. Most of all I hated the way he brought
a smile to Pat. She was my Patty, not his
except ,she wasn't. She thought Ray was the
bees' knees. After that every word out of
Patty's mouth was Ray did this Ray said
this.... RAY, RAY, RAY!!!

What a fire extinguisher. How I hated that
name. He was a cake-eater, making a play
for every woman near him; but did Pat see
that? She did not! She cast a kitten, when I
brought it up and accused me of lying and
being jealous. Hell yes, I was jealous; but I
didn't lie.

I was dizzy for the dame, but Sergeant Ray
Walters wormed his way into Pat's heart.
She forgot all about me. Some say I should
have been more forgiving and thought only
of her happiness; but I really believed I was
he was a crumb bum. I knew he was; the
world just didn't know it and was my turn to
prove it. Ray might have the bulge, but I had
the muscles and Ray would go down if he
was who I thought he was and if he was a
good guy then he'd have my blessing and I
back off. Patsy deserved happiness even if it
wasn't with me.

I started investigating the guy. Scouting him wasn't easy. I had to dress up like a sweet patootie. Even my own dearly departed mom wouldn't have recognized me. I was a looker, a hot mama, if those wolf whistles, I got walking down the street were anything to go by. I sought my quarry and watched him pretending to be a good time girl, hoping he wouldn't run me in. It wouldn't look good on my rap sheet.

I watched like a hawk, as he patrolled the street. I saw him rough up a couple of no-good torpedoes. a hustle them off to some cells. He gave some jaywalking tickets to some very pissed off citizens. My surveillance was not paying off.

This should have made me back off, but it made me more determined. Ray was dirty! I knew it! I watched him for another week; toning down the costume ,I wore I dressed as an older woman, a bum off the street. I looked hideous with blackened teeth and a smell that would chase a dog away. He'd never recognize me and neither would Patty, if I came across her.

I spotted the asshole taking bribes and
pulling out my camera. I clicked off a few
shots, got some he didn't notice; but the last
one I took where the dame we all knew as
the mayor's wife kissed him and gave him
the cash .His eyes opened in shock. The
flash alerted him though and he ran after me
I barely made it into a building ;where I had
hidden my real clothes. There I dispensed
with my get-up and hid out until the
goombah left. I went to my rooms developed
the shots and I then took my pictures to the
district attorney and internal affairs. They
put the pinch on him. Ha, ha!

 I had to testify and for awhile Pat was
madder than a hen at me. My abundant
charm however won her over .that and the
fourteen-carat diamond she wore on her
finger as a promise that come next month,
we'd marry. (I'd had to work day and night
for some bigwig to earn the dough for six
months, but it was worth it)

A short time later and I showed her my
wedding present to her. They'll be no more
women tricking this P.I. I've got a partner
now and the name on the door in gold
lettering is Jack and Pat Forbes Private
Investigators.

If you enjoyed this story read more of Jack's adventures in Jack be Nimble on sale at Amazon and your favorite realtor.

~0~

Chapter 1 Excerpt from A Penny Saved A Murder Earned

Book 1 of the Kelly Murder Mysteries

Chapter 1 – Bloody Shoes

"A penny saved is a penny earned" ~ *Benjamin Franklin*

T he blood streaked across the floor, but

he had carefully sidestepped it. Stupid bitch! She got what she deserved. How dare she defile his Angel's property? He hadn't left a trace...had he? No, he was too clever by half.

A voice he didn't recognize interrupted his thoughts, "I didn't spot you entering.

Working late, dear? Of course, I forgot; you have an early opening tomorrow."

The man strode closer to the killer and the body lying on the floor, "Wait a minute, you aren't the lady. Who are you? You shouldn't be here," the man continued clearly alarmed.

"You shouldn't be here either," the murderer insisted.

"You, you killed Megan. I'm telling."

"Really? You know this was something you shouldn't be allowed to see."

"I'm leaving. I didn't notice anything," the man lied, witnessing the blood.

"I'm sorry pal. Wrong place, wrong time!" the killer answered.

The homeless man ran dodging racks, finally deciding to hide behind some shelving. The killer ran after him, puzzled for a moment because he could see no trace of the homeless person. The murderer then laughed, as he realized how foolish the vagrant was being, his stench gave him away. He subdued the man with a Taser gun. Waiting seconds. he then pulled the man from his hiding place. Taking ties from within his pocket; he fastened the man's arms and feet. Satisfied that the homeless person was now trussed up like a turkey, he smiled.

"P...P....P...Please! I don't want to die!" the man cried, visibly sweating and starting to shake.

The man tried to kick out his legs and arms but failed.

"You've heard about fate? Well sorry but this is your fate, buddy!" the murderer explained.

"P...P...P...Please, I'm begging you! Couldn't you let me go? I won't tell! I'll move to another city. Besides who would listen to a homeless man?"

"Someone would. My Angel would."

The homeless man then smiled as if to gain trust from this killer, "You won't hurt the lady who owns the store, will you?" he asked.

"I would never harm my Angel. How dare you?" the killer responded outraged.

"S...S...S...Sorry! I didn't mean to insult you! Please just let me go. I'm harmless ask anyone...."

"What is your name?"

"Why do you need my name?" He asked looking puzzled then reconsidering he answered, "My name is Al."

The killer put his gloves back on and smoothed them and then turned his back on his victim.

"You're going to kill me now. Aren't you? Just don't harm the sweet lady who owns this store. Will it hurt?" the man asked resigned.

"I would never hurt my Angel. She is sweet, isn't she? Unfortunately, that also makes unscrupulous people take advantage of her."

"I promise I would never take advantage of her kindness. I wouldn't!!! She's the best part of my day and this city, Happy Valley, Ontario. She picked me up from the gutter and helped me."

"I know you wouldn't and it hurts me to do this. Tell you what though, I'll make your death painless because I like you, Al," the

killer offered, feeling suddenly sorry for the
man. Then he checked himself. Living on
the streets was hell; maybe he was doing the
guy a favour? Yes, of course he was. Taking
a pill bottle out of his pocket and opening
the dispenser, he placed some in a coffee
cup he took from the sideboard. He filled the
cup with the tepid coffee from the coffee
pot, stirring the pills in rapidly.

"C...c...c...couldn't you let me go? I won't
tell and I'll watch over her when you're not
here."

"Sorry, times up, Al. Here now, drink this
coffee," the assassin commanded placing the
mug at Al's lips.

Al tried not to drink and spit some of the
coffee out, but the assassin plugged his nose
and the cup was soon empty.

"Admit it Al, you had a crappy life. Just
give in and go to the light. I hear good
things wait there for people like you," the
killer stated.

Al tried to fight some more, but he soon
found it was losing battle. Al's breathing
slowed as he slipped into a deep sleep and
stopped breathing altogether. His age and
living on the streets made the pills work fast.

Now what to do with the body? The killer thought. His Angel must not find this man's remains here, bad enough he left Megan's body here for his Angel to find. He couldn't hide Megan though she needed to be found. Every needed to know she suffered for her crime. Maybe even his Angel would see Megan's evil and protect herself from people like that. This man, Al however knew his Angel and she cared about him. It was so like her to look after the homeless. He could let her cry over Al. Where could he put the man so he wouldn't be found?

The dumpster of course...the perfect place for Al! The day after tomorrow was garbage day. Covered in garbage no one would find Al.

~0~

The next day

Lily

Ominous clouds replaced the

morning's sunlight, turning the skies to shades of deep purple, and navy blue, streaked with gray. Lily Kelly stared at the sky for moment, and then departed the courthouse doors in Happy Valley, Ontario, Canada, skipping down the steps. The city looked its age of over a hundred as the buildings downtown looked old and decrepit. If only the town could find some money to fix downtown Lily thought.

Then her mind turned to Amelia, her cousin and best friend. Amelia ,needed Lily to support her in her grief. Lily had a fight with her husband Horace again this morning, about how much time he was spending at the office and how much time she spent supporting Amelia. Lily was always working, and so was Horace, so how much time was Rose their fourteen-year-old daughter really getting?

Lily had won in court, but all she could think about was her family. Everyone needed her and she felt like she was being pulled in three different directions. Something had to give and it looked like it was her job. She would have to cut back on some of her work. Her family had to come first.

Lily stumbled some more over the steps only stopping from hurrying across the courtyard to her office, when her heel broke on her shoe. Today was supposed to be about her victory after her win in court; but it appeared with her expensive shoe's heel breaking, she was mistaken. They ought to get the ruts in the paving stones fixed; that was her reflection as she cursed her bad break. What did they say about omens? Maybe she should have taken a hint from the heavens' darkening? She noted as her bad luck had seemed to get worse with the arrival of some reporters.

"Ms. Kelly, give us a statement about the Rockwood case?" yelled one reporter.

"Ms. Kelly, how does the Sulimani family feel about your victory?" yelled another.

One bold reporter stepped forward, "Crown Attorney Kelly, congratulations on your win. Was it hard to try a case which involved a council member?" asked Paul Knight from the local television station, thrusting a microphone in Lily's face.

"Anyone who commits a crime in Happy Valley will be tried by the Crown with the full force of the law, despite their office. So no, I did not find it difficult to do my job," Lily replied testily.

"Thank you, Ms. Kelly. What does the Sulimani family think about the judgement?"

"Amani Sulimani was five-years old, when Zebadiah Rockwood's truck went through a red light. His truck struck the back of the Sulimani's SUV killing her. He then left the scene pursued by good Samaritans, who wished to stop Mr. Rockwood from continuing driving drunk: a pursuit caused by Mr. Rockwood's actions, which put a number of lives in danger."

"Will the family be comforted with this conviction?" queried another reporter.

"Amani Sulimani existed as their only child. Mr. Rockwood's conviction will not bring her back, but hopefully will bring some peace of mind to her family knowing he will be behind bars." Lily answered.

"Do you sense, given your own personal tragedies that you'll be able to get a sentence fitting the crime?"

"My family's history does not come into my trial cases, only the person's guilt."

"And when will sentencing take place?" asked another reporter.

"Sentencing will take place next month."

"Thank you, Ms. Kelly. This is Paul Knight reporting, with an update on the Zebadiah Rockwood's drunken driving case. Zebadiah Rockwood was a long-time council member here in Happy Valley. He took a leave of absence to deal with his legal issues. Mr. Rockwood was charged with impaired driving causing death, two counts of failing to remain at the scene of an accident and dangerous driving last December. When asked about the conviction today Mr. Rockwood and his lawyer issued a no comment. We will have the complete story for you at six pm. Paul Knight reporting for CHPV-TV."

Lily hated speaking on camera, even though it was part of her job as the Crown attorney, so she was glad the scrum had been completed.

She hated sounding tough and unyielding but it was all in the description of her job title. She had fought difficult challenges to get this job and she had to work hard and fight hard to keep it. After all there were aspects of her job she loved like putting the bad people that would harm others away. The press was gone and she was now free to go to her office to file her reports and leave early. She crossed the street, entered her building and went straight up to her office.

"Victory is mine!" Lily Kelly cried triumphantly as she walked into her office.

"So, you won?" asked Colleen Finn, her administrative assistant.

"Yes, I bested that idiot, Michael Taylor. He thought he would beat me in court. He actually believed his client would win."

"Good for you, boss, I knew you would nail his lily-white ass to the wall. He's such a scumbag lawyer all his clients seem to be as guilty as hell."

"Colleen! Language! But thank-you," Lily answered, showing pearly white teeth.

Colleen looked expectantly at Lily and she felt stupid did she miss something? Oh, the joke! Lily hadn't laughed at Colleen's wit.

"Funny, I got it. Zebadiah Rockwood's sentencing takes place next month, but he will be held until then; no bail, no goodbyes to his favourite watering hole. As the Crown, I'll recommend the longest sentence I can get that he can serve. It's victories like these which make my job worthwhile. I don't know how much satisfaction this will give that little girl's family, but at least they'll know her killer remains in jail. He can't take another life again, because he will be incarcerated."

Lily went over to her desk and sat down.

"Can you imagine Michael Taylor, tried to use the defence that Rockwood was not drunk. Just tired? He claimed Rockwood drank only after the accident, while driving his company's truck; so, the company couldn't possibly be responsible,"

"I believe you told me that before," Colleen commented, "However I'm glad you proved he'd drank so much before getting in the truck. That proved he was legally under the influence when the accident occurred. I hope I was some help in that aspect."

"Yes, you were invaluable."

"Thanks, Lily."

"It's still early; only nine forty-five, and my day's clear until what, two-thirty?"

"That's correct." Colleen replied.

Colleen checked a day planner, frowning, "Is everything okay, Lily? You seem a little down."

"Everything is fine. Amelia's grand opening starts at noon, but I promised to be there sooner if possible. If I go right now, I'll surprise her," Lily grabbed her coat to leave.

"I'm glad she's doing so well. Although after what happened, Amelia needs the encouragement. Please tell her, I'll try to get to her store another day. I hope her store has great success."

"Thank-you, I will tell Amelia. Hold all my calls Colleen. Unless it's urgent then call my cell."

"I'll do that. What time should I say you'll be back?" Colleen responded to a departing Lily.

"Tell whoever asks that I'll be back after two p.m..."

"And if they ask where you are?" Colleen questioned.

"Tell them I'm meeting with a witness," Lily replied with a wink.

"If there's cake bring me back a piece. Please, boss?" Colleen begged.

"I ordered a cake, but it's not supposed to arrive until one thirty so we'll see. I'm leaving now. Remember only urgent calls to my cell phone." Lily cautioned, leaving through the front door.

She twisted her shimmering brown hair back up into its traditional bun. Pulling out her cell phone, she dialled Amelia's store. There was no answer. How odd! Amelia must be busy putting out last minute stock.

~0~

~0~

A few minutes ago

lone male walked into the store.

His left hand held a gun while his right hand steadied it. He strode in with caution. His dark brown eyes dart from corner to corner, searching for an assailant. His well over six-foot tall frame slouched. Ruggedly handsome, with dark brown hair clipped short to his head; he was dressed in a dark blue jacket and dress pants; a badge is also clipped to his belt buckle. Finding the scene secure he putting his gun away and pulled a pair of gloves out of his suit coat pocket and a pair of booties, which he slipped on his shoes.

He checked the victim. No pulse. Advancing forward, he bent down to check the second woman; her phone still in her hand, her head bloody. He noted the second victim was still breathing, though unconscious. He looked around, as if waiting for someone. Deciding they weren't coming yet; he took out a mini recorder. He started scanning the scene and speaking aloud.

"This is Sergeant Detective Emmett Rogers. I am at the scene of a homicide, at Quirks, one forty-five Maple Street. A woman lays sprawled out across the floor. The woman's arms are positioned underneath her, as if to break her fall.

The back of her head and her long blonde hair are streaked in rusty-brown blood, as well as her clothing below the hair. Blood pools across the floor spiralling out in two long streams. Footprints are noticeable, as if someone stepped through the drying blood. The weapon appears to be a pair of scissors, found beneath the victim. I have marked both of these."

The man spoke aloud as he walked around, carefully avoiding contaminating the evidence, by stepping over a paper cup.

"A coffee cup... possibly one of those lattes is overturned. I'm sure the forensics team can determine this if necessary. Its contents are also spilled on the floor and countertop. Coffee is spilled at the front door and possibly on the shoes. The second victim's shoes are not on the bruised victim, but on the floor. The shoes can be found near an overturned ladder, at the front door. It appears the woman, who appears unconscious, may have been carrying a ladder and toy stock to place on the shelves, when she slipped in the blood.

The man paused to think.

"This might be a setup by the second victim to cover the actual crime. The woman, however, seems to have the victim's blood all over her clothes and hands like she crawled through the blood. I believe there are two possible scenarios here. One the owner of the shop, one Amelia Kelly (the unconscious person), murdered her employee or unknown victim and set this up to appear a perpetrator broke in and killed her accidentally hurting herself in the process.

Or two... it is at it now seems that she stumbled on the crime scene and harmed herself."

He pulled out a notebook again and examined the room taking some more taking notes.

"Is it a robbery gone wrong? It is too soon to tell. The store owner will be en-route to hospital as soon as the EMTs have arrived. Interview to follow. The time is now ten twenty a.m.," he concluded turning off his recorder.

He examined the room scribbling on his notepad.

~0~

Now

Lily and Detective Emmett Rogers

The man's eyes turned and his vision focused completely. A woman entered the store. His eyes took in her tall and slender form and her long shimmering brown hair, pulled into a tight roll. He noted she was closely followed by the Emergency technicians and gave a sigh of relief. The woman entering the store had brilliant blue eyes. He had a feeling she often turned heads, even dressed as she was, in her business attire. But he noted something about the way she walked screamed money and upper class.

"Oh no, Amelia!" she screamed and tried to rush to Amelia, but was stopped by the man's arm.

"This is a crime scene ma'am. We don't want you disrupting our evidence. Let the EMTs and detectives do their job. Then you can go to ...you're er...friend?" Sergeant Detective Rogers commanded.

"Crime scene? What has happened?" Lily asked politely, wanting to be cooperative.

"Ma'am, I'll know better after I assess the scene. Until then, please remain near the front door." ordered Detective Rogers briskly.

"I promise I'll stay out of the way; but at least can I get her Adrienne Changs?"

"What or who, are Adrienne Changs?" said Detective Rogers looking totally perplexed.

"Shoes, those shoes right there!" Lily pointed to a pair of heels lying behind the yellow tape.

"You're worried about shoes? Woman! Do you have any idea of what's going on here?" Detective Rogers snapped, shaking his head.

"You, sexist pig!" countered Lily under her breath, "Men!" Losing her temper now and louder she continued, "Those shoes are worth five hundred dollars! And she probably wore them for what, a half an hour? And you want me to walk away and leave them to be destroyed in some kind of liquid!"

"Liquid that's blood! And five hundred dollars for shoes? Is she crazy?" Detective Rogers asked dumfounded.

"No! She's not crazy. How dare you?" Lily asked suddenly outraged.

He was smug, wasn't he? Handsome yes, but oh so smug, she questioned herself. That wasn't important. Amelia was injured on the floor and he questioned her? Instead of letting her go to her cousin! What was wrong with Lily? Why was she so worried and focused on the shoes? They were only shoes. Amelia was injured; who cared about footwear?

"Sorry, ma'am, the shoes are evidence now. Name? Occupation? Address?" Detective Rogers barked, ignoring her statement.

"I want to see your identification first, and then you'll get the information," insisted Lily.

"I am Sergeant Detective Emmett Rogers," the man revealed, showing his police badge.

"Oh, that's funny," Lily uttered laughing, "If you and Amelia were introduced it would be Aem and Em."

Lily followed this up by hysterically laughing and then alternatively crying. What was wrong with her? She never lost it like this. She always appeared a professional. She had seen crime scenes. She could handle this. Couldn't she? Amelia would be okay. Wouldn't she?!

"Get a hold of yourself Lily. You have embarrassed yourself," Lily heard this voice in her head, she recognized as her father's. Odd, how her dad's voice, came back to her now, she rarely saw him, since he lived in

Prague and he only called about twice a year.

"Ma'am, what you are saying is not remotely funny. Are you all, right? Put your head between your knees if you feel lightheaded. I think your friend's relatively fine. She might have a head injury and possibly a broken leg, but she'll be okay." Sergeant Detective Rogers then turned to the Emergency technicians (EMTs) to seek confirmation demanded, "Right?"

"Should be. But head injuries can be serious," the one EMT replied.

Sergeant Detective Rogers shot him a disapproving look.

"Yes, the Sergeant Detective is right. She'll be fine. She'll be taken to the hospital for treatment," the Emergency Technician agreed, finally.

"See...what did I tell you? Now that we have that out of the way; I need to see some identification and then get some answers to my questions. Name? Address? Occupation?

The reason you are here?" Detective Rogers barked at Lily.

"Amelia's my best friend and more. This should have been the greatest day of her life, her opening of her new store; a one of kind toy and collectibles retailer. A grand opening and now it's ruined. Who did this to her?" Lily asked, uncharacteristically wringing her hands and still trying to regain her calm, as thoughts of Amelia's demise threatened to enter her mind.

"Ma'am, she slipped in blood. She hit her head on the floor and on the ladder. No one harmed her. She did this to herself," explained Sergeant Detective Rogers.

"I realize she's clumsy, but she didn't put blood there to trip in," defended Lily angrily.

"No, the blood was spilled by whoever killed the woman behind the counter."

"Someone is dead behind the counter?" Lily responded shocked and surprised.

"No comment; as I explained Ma'am this is an active crime scene. Now as I asked before what is your name?" Detective Rogers insisted forcefully again.

"Lily Kelly-Brooksfield. My husband is Horace Brooksfield, the mayor. We live down the street on Beaconfield. Do you want the number? It's nine hundred and sixty-two." she replied condescendingly.

"If you're Mayor Brooksfield's wife... then you're the Crown Attorney." Coming to this realization, Sergeant Detective Rogers hid a sigh.

"Please update me on this active crime scene, now," commanded Lily pulling back her shoulders.

Emmett Rogers put on his professional face and smiled. The smile was just so warm and inviting that Lily felt warm all over. Lily frowned back at him; she was just felt so angry. This cop who grinned back at her was the biggest reason. She was a married woman. She shouldn't be attracted to a cop who apparently existed to give her grief and solve a murder. She threw back her shoulders again. It was okay to look at someone attractive, she excused herself. Everyone looks, and most of the time it meant nothing. It's only if you acted on any attraction, it became wrong. She would never act on the temptation. Besides he appeared to be the most annoying man she'd ever met.

"Ma'am, you know I can't fill you in on any of this case. You'll have to recuse yourself from this case, as you're familiar with the crime scene." Detective Rogers emphasized, once again interrupting Lily's thoughts.

"Why don't you just come out and say what you think. You consider me a suspect," Lily uttered.

"A lot of people are suspects in my book. I have to make a case for them committing the crime or I have to eliminate them as suspects. And don't attempt to solve this yourself; amateurs just get in the way." Detective Rogers explained, his eyes wandering.

Lily was slightly amused. Detective Rogers thought she wanted to insinuate herself into this murder investigation? She might not have before that comment, but she did now. He seemed to be focusing on Amelia or Lily as his prime suspect. Lily knew neither of them had committed this murder, so that meant she had no choice but to find out for herself who had committed this crime.

She would pretend she wanted nothing to do with this situation, even as far as passing it off to her underling Barbara. After all she could always investigate behind the scenes.

Spotting the emergency technicians Detective Rogers exclaimed "Oh good, the ambulance has arrived to take the victim to the hospital. Now can we can get down to brass tacks; you can fill me in on these people and anything else you know or have held back from me."

"I want to go with her," Lily protested.

Lily pulled herself back taking several steps back putting distance between herself and this cop. It was odd, how alive she felt when she jousted with him. He was a cop investigating a murder and she was married.

"Stop this now Lily!" She told herself.

"Ma'am, I realize you want to go see your friend. Before I could release you from the scene, I need something from you. We need you to identify the other victim. Maybe you'll recognize her when I turn over the body." Detective Rogers explained, softening a little, as he slipped on another pair of gloves.

"Only if you'll stop calling me Ma'am. Call me Lily or Crown Attorney Kelly, but not Ma'am. It makes me feel eighty years old."

"If it will get you to identify the victim...thank-you Crown Attorney Kelly."

"Let's look, shall we?" Lily agreed.

Lily took a breath as she gathered herself to observe who lay there dead. She gasped as she stared over the counter to see the back of the woman's head. She covered her mouth in horror.

"Good grief! I never realized they appear so alike from the back," replied Lily shocked.

"Who do you think she looks like ma'am?" demanded Detective Rogers.

"What did I say about ma'am? Don't they give you sensitivity training at Police College? You want to know who this is? This is Megan, Megan Fowler. She's an employee of Amelia's. But she works evenings she's...is.... was a college student. I can't believe this is Megan. Megan is such a sweet girl and worked part-time to be able to go to school and support her mother. Why would someone kill her? Do you think it's possible someone mistook her for Amelia?" Lily rambled, tears slipping from her eyes.

"That's a possibility, ma'am. We will explore all aspects."

"I know the drill, Sergeant Detective Rogers." Lily gave the detective a mock salute, "Why can't you admit that they mistook Megan for Amelia?"

"We don't have any of the facts yet, Ms. Kelly," replied Detective Rogers.

"What about Amelia? Is she in any danger?" asked Lily.

"If I were to speculate, I suppose that could be a possibility," Detective Rogers answered non-committally.

They both watched as the technicians gathered the evidence and blood samples and took pictures before the body was taken away.

"Will someone be assigned to guard her and keep her safe?" Lily asked getting exasperated.

"That's in motion, Crown Attorney Kelly," Detective Rogers explained, trying not to sound annoyed that she's telling him how to do his job.

Detective Rogers and Lily turned as another cop swaggered into the store. Burly and well over six feet tall, his hair was dark like Detective Rogers. Unlike Detective Rogers, this man preened like a peacock; Lily was aware of the type.

Guys like him smiled with their mouths and not their eyes. They thought all women should admire them and only them. She noted his smile went as far as his lips.

"What have you got here, Emmett?"

"Nothing you need to be concerned about, Brad," Detective Rogers replied, obvious tension showing between the two.

"You should be able to get some great publicity out of this one," Brad said loudly to Detective Rogers.

Brad then strutted over to the murder scene.

"It's my case, Brad," Detective Rogers insisted.

"I'm not trying to interfere," Brad persisted walking around, "I just thought if you needed some help, I would lend a hand. It doesn't look like something you could handle on your own."

"I don't need help, thanks, Brad. I don't need you messing up my crime scene." Detective Rogers declared "I've got it all under control.

"It doesn't look that way to me. I would solve this case quickly. You could use me in your corner," Brad continued.

"We don't need you. Now the Crown attorney is here, so I have it all in hand. Goodbye, Brad." Detective Rogers practically spat.

"Ah, the lovely Crown attorney Kelly is here. Can't go now," Brad exclaimed trying to sound charming but failing miserably.

"And you are?" asked Lily putting her full aristocratic chill in to her voice.

"I'm Brad Owens, at your service, Attorney Kelly. Sergeant Detective Brad Owens. I use to be Emmett's partner," Brad explained smiling and pointing to Detective Rogers.

Detective Rogers rolled his eyes. "Thank God, you're not anymore," He stated under his breath loud enough for only he and Lily to hear.

"So. what do you think, Crown Attorney? Was it a robbery gone wrong?" asked Brad.

"I'm not sure. Why do I bother to tell you this? This isn't your case," Lily commented suddenly not willing to share with Brad.

She didn't know why. Something about his smile, and the way Emmett Rogers had reacted to him made her dislike him. Brad's smile was phony, like a used car salesman. It was slick and slimy. That wasn't fair to used car sales people. Lily was sure they were more honest than this phoney, Brad Owens. Lily had come across a lot of people in her job. She certainly felt she was a good judge of character. In fact, she could spot a phoney a mile away.

Detective Emmett Rogers, unlike Brad Owens, appeared like he knew his job. She'd heard of him many times, but had never run into him on the job until today. Thank goodness for the Internet on her phone. He was a dedicated cop. He had done his time and had come up through the ranks, strictly on merit. Detective Rogers didn't seem to like Brad Owens and that was reason enough for Lily not to trust him.

Emmett Rogers had an exemplary record as a police officer; she trusted his instincts and knowledge over this smarmy, Detective Brad Owens. He'd get to the bottom of this. Lily wished he would let her leave soon and check on Amelia. They had spent their teen years together and were as close as sisters. She'd always felt responsible for Amelia, being two years older. She wanted to make sure Amelia was okay.

"Okay. Well, if you don't need my help, I'm leaving because I have work to do. There are other crimes to investigate." Brad answered leaving, "See you around Emmett."

"Not if I see you first," muttered Emmett under his breath.

"So, am I free to go?" Lily demanded.

Emmett then offered her his pen.

"I have your address, so as long as you sign here in my notebook. "You are free to go," he said gesturing.

Lily glanced over at Detective Owens and watched him leave before reaching for the book. She then signed her signature with a flourish. Detective Rogers scanned the signature, thinking momentarily, it was just as elegant as Lily. He shook his head, reminding himself to stay connected to reality.

"So, I am free to go, Detective?" Lily repeated.

"I'll be checking in on your friend, of course, and I may need to follow-up with you later, but as of now, you are free to go." he smiled, already exhausted.

"I would expect nothing else from you, Detective Rogers."

As she got into her car, Lily breathed a sigh of relief she had finally been able to leave the store. She buckled up her seatbelt and put her car in gear.

Backing the car up, Lily pulled out into the street and narrowly missed getting hit by a car, she didn't view. Luckily the other driver slammed on his brakes. She noticed the male driver shouting, "Stupid woman driver" as she read his lips in her rear-view mirror. He was justified in his anger. It had been her fault, but she didn't have time to dwell.

She headed down the road toward the hospital; despite her resolve her mind wandered. She thought about poor Megan's mother getting the news of her daughter's death. It would kill Lily to get news like that about her adopted daughter, Rose.

What kind of monster kills a young woman? Why did, whomever it was, have to kill Megan? It wasn't a robbery, she'd read in Detective Rogers' notes, when he gave his notebook to her to sign her statement. As Lily drove, more questions flooded into her head. Was Amelia the real target? Megan certainly appeared like Amelia from the back.

Amelia didn't appear too hurt. Maybe she suffered a concussion? Concussions could be serious; she knew from her readings. The EMT hadn't said Amelia was in serious condition though. Not that the EMT could explain before Emmett Rogers got on his case.

Revving the engine, she waited impatiently for the light to go green. Once Lily reached the hospital, she could reassure herself, Amelia was all right.

~0~

Excerpt from Love's Labour's Won
Preface:

<u>Love's Labour's Won</u>

Sarah sought a job,

Biting back a sob,

Her love and life,

All constant strife,

And filled with unbroken sorrow,

Like there was no tomorrow.

She thought her future,

Safely to be assured,

Instead of that Sarah found,

Many wonders to astound,

The world changed forever,

Yet the pull of a tether,

For the prize she sought,

And the joy and pain it wrought,

And all that she had done,

Was "Love's Labour's Won"

By S.G. Lee

~-0~

Except From Love's Labour's Won

Chapter 1 - Want Ads

Life was getting Sarah down. She was

twenty-one years old and what did she have to show for it? Did she have a career? No, she didn't. Did life produce a boyfriend, husband or children? Another no! Or even a significant other? She had no one, no one to care if she lived or died. She had worked so many dead-end jobs; too many to count.

She had once been a Wal-Mart Greeter and even spent a winter as a telemarketer selling lawn services for the upcoming spring. She failed miserably not making that job a success either. Numerous hang-ups ensued and no sales.

They kept her for a month and then said… "I'm sorry you're not working out."

Like, duh. She didn't complete any sales. She had to make a living somehow.

She scanned the want ads. There remained lots of jobs for coffee servers, but she was so tired of smiling and serving food to people. Then she spotted the ad, the ad which made her sit up and take notice.

Companion wanted.

Must be young presentable and personable.

Apply by phone at 555-5555 only serious inquires need apply.

Must have two references

What was this some kind of weird scam luring young woman to their peril? Really, how dramatic was she being?

Sarah normally ignored such an ad, but she was getting short on cash and the rent was due next week.

She didn't have the eight hundred and fifty dollars the landlord wanted for this dump…err…wonderful furnished apartment. She'd be out on the street if she didn't earn some money. It wasn't like she had a lot of friends, which she could ask to crash on their sofas. Melanie would have let her, but she was off on a modeling job in France. Melanie had sublet her apartment to a yuppie couple that obviously didn't know Sarah.

Should I or shouldn't I call? Sarah thought. I mean was it safe? What if the employers subsisted as white slavers? The people Gran were always warning her about growing up? Gran's notions bordered on the ridiculous, of course. So, I should just seize the opportunity. Sarah thought. Gran was gone and so were her worrisome and outdated ideas. Sarah looked at the ads again.

Barista wanted must have previous experience and two references.

Must be prepared to clean and carry up to 40 pounds of product.

The ad's specifications were a new take on the job. They were warning people that they would be heavy lifting. Hmm, generally they told you this when you started the job. But forty pounds, what the heck?

Were they having the baristas carry coffee beans? There had to be another job offer somewhere in these online sites. She scanned the ads once again.

No nothing in the ads but a companion job.
A companion job didn't sound so bad. Did
it? She needed a job and jobs were scarce
that she qualified for right now. She had to
at least try to get the job, didn't she? She
took a huge breath and dialled the number.

"Hello," the voice said on the other end of
the line.

A real live person answered instead of the
answering machine Sarah expected. Sarah
took another deep breath.

"Uh I'd like to apply for the job; you placed
in the Free Press." She replied with all the
enthusiasm she could muster.

"I see… and what makes you believe you're
the person we are looking for?" Asked the
voice on the other end of the line

"I like people and people like me. I am often
stopped by strangers and they always seem
compelled to tell me their complete life
histories," Sarah replied.

"Uh huh, and how do you respond to these
indignities to your peace and quiet?" asked
the voice.

"I am aware not everyone would listen; I find it fascinating to hear the stories people tell and to just listen if that's what they need. In some way I feel I can help them. It's not an intrusion," Sarah answered without even thinking.

"I comprehend one such as you, may have led a very difficult life. People do not always return the kindness to that you seem to offer so freely. You are an old soul," replied the voice sounding distinctively male, and little too familiar.

"Well…I don't know if this is odd or what but a long time ago, I decided I liked me. If others find me a Pollyanna; a person who is too kind, too naive for the world, that's their problem. I like being different even if others think me odd, I can only be me. Oh, I can't believe I'm telling you this, in a job interview no less. Now you'll never hire me and I'm sorry I've wasted your time, sir." Sarah responded embarrassed and about to hang up.

"Miss, please don't hang up. I think you are an excellent potential candidate for this rather unique job."

"You think I might be the person you want?" asked Sarah incredulously.

"Well clearly my employer would have the final say, but you sound as if you might make my short list of candidates."

"Not to make you mad or anything and lose my chance at this job; but don't you think you should know more about me?"

"I am a very good judge of character. That's why my employer trusts me in this manner," stated the man with an almost mesmerizing voice. Sarah felt herself believing every word he said.

"Wow, you must be in a prestigious job," replied Sarah without thinking again.

"The only possible drawback to your employment might be your tendency to forthcoming with your thoughts. Do you do this often Miss?"

"Miss Sarah Dexler, and no I don't usually blurt out everything. There is simply something about you."

Sarah realized her blunder. "Sorry I'm doing it again I don't know what has come over me. I promise I'm not typically like this and would guard myself with your employer."

"Never fear Miss Dexler. I'm a good judge of character and you seem to be nice and kind. My employer needs kindness, and someone who will listen most of all. You said you do that with strangers. You listen and help others, so that makes you a candidate we simply must see."

The man suddenly sounded very interested and in the next second, he surprised Sarah with, "So would you be available for an interview tomorrow at 3 PM?"

"Yes, of course," Sarah became tentative. "I guess I could."

"Obviously given the generalities of our ad some applicants have been taken back and would like assurances of our trust worthiness. My employer, though he wishes to remain anonymous until the candidates are found, will be quite happy to provide references for himself. Confidentiality agreements are signed as well. These, of course, will be provided at the interview stage. Interviews will be conducted at our temporary office at 1000 Park Street. We look forward to seeing you there, Miss

Dexler. Goodbye," the man ended the call
abruptly.

Sarah closed her cell phone and thought…
how strange this man appeared so
mesmerizing on the phone He even seemed
to snatch thoughts from her head. It was all a
bit odd. Then as she thought some more, she
realized even stranger he had forgotten to
share his name. Had she distracted the poor
man? Why had he forgotten to share his
name? His English upper crust accent
sounded so prim, proper and professional it
seemed even peculiar to her now that he did
not reveal his name. Still, she hoped this job
would pan out or in a few days she'd be
begging on the street corner.

~0~

Chapter 2 - Venimus, Vidimus, Vicimus

Sarah was in a hurry. She tried on every

outfit she owned for this interview. Most of her wardrobe now lay strewn across her bed or floor. She finally settled on this black pantsuit. The tailored jacket was flattering and her pants that went with the jacket, sculpted her rear end. Not that was necessary in an interview, but it gave her a lift. She felt like a model in this outfit. A tall shapely model, because of these four-inch heels on her black sandals. They had cost her quite a fortune, when she was pulling in a pay cheque, but they were worth every penny. Sarah felt beautiful and hoped her confidence, would translate into a job. She really needed this job.

She entered the door at one thousand Park Street. The building was one of those non-descript glass buildings ,with about forty floors. She entered the building and realized the man on the phone, had not given her the office number, only the building number address. Without the office number ,she was lost. She could take the elevator ,but to where?

Sarah was in near tears, thinking maybe the whole conversation with that man was a joke, a terrible joke on her. She spent her last five dollars to take a cab, so she wouldn't be late. She was lost.... the job was lost. Oh no, even worse she'd be out on the street in a few days.

No, she couldn't let that happen. She had told the man on the phone she was good with people. That she could charm total strangers into telling their stories, so here was the time to prove it. She'd find the office. It might take a little talking; asking people questions that would lead to the office number. But surely being late would be excused ,when he realized he forgot to tell her the office number. Sarah began by talking to the receptionist at the desk in the hallway. She approached the young woman and she was almost taken aback. The receptionist appeared gorgeous her hair a beautiful honey blonde and cascading down in corkscrew ringlets. The receptionist's bright blue eyes, were like diamonds and red lipstick finished the face, that could launch a thousand ships. She was dressed in a very tight red dress. It didn't seem quite appropriate for the office, but who was Sarah to judge? Sarah couldn't help, but wonder if this was the type of beauty that they hired here if so, she was in trouble. She couldn't compete with someone so incredibly lovely, or wear those oh, so, revealing clothes.

"Hi, my name is Sarah. I have a little problem .I'm hoping that someone as knowledgeable and as intelligent as you are, could help me with," Sarah began.

"That's so flattering , that you think I can help you. People tend to treat me like a bit of an airhead ;because I'm a receptionist .It's my job to assist people. I guess my parents didn't do me any favours, by naming me Brandy," babbled Brandy, breathlessly while snapping her gum.

"Oh, your name is Brandy? You know, some say Brandy is better than fine wine," Sarah piled on the charm.

"I'm not... you know…. so, if …you know if that's what this is all about you can stop right there. Nothing against your preferences, but I'm seeing a guy," replied Brandy awkwardly misunderstanding.

"Oh no….no …. Really, there's nothing to worry about. I am straight too. I'm here trying to get a job. You see, I applied for this job, but the man on the phone, forgot to tell me the office number where the interview is," explained Sarah.

"That's difficult, because there's tons of offices in this building. Do you know what the guy looks like?" asked Brandy looking at her red painted fingernails and sliding a nail file over them.

"Sadly no, you see I talked to the man on the phone. He had an upper crust British accent though. Does that help you identify him for me?" begged Sarah.

"Oh, you are so in luck today." Brandy replied, "We have only one guy who talks like that here. Mr. Poundstone. He's conducting interviews today, too, so, he is probably your man."

"Oh, thank you so much Brandy, you don't know how much this means to me. Oh, wait a minute I have a coupon for a free coffee, here this for you," answered Sarah, digging the coupon out of her purse.

"But if you're looking for a job, you must need the coupon."

"I wanted to let you know how much I truly, appreciated your help," Sarah insisted sincerely.

"You are a really nice person, Sarah; I hope you get the job. Maybe we can share a coffee break when you do. You know... if you end up working in this building. Now the office number for Mr. Poundstone is 304. And just because I want you to get the job, if anyone asks for the number, because he forgot to tell them I won't tell them," Brandy insisted winking.

"Oh no, that wouldn't be right," asserted Sarah, although delighted. "If they ask, please tell them. If this job is meant to be, I'll get the position."

"Did anyone ever tell you Sarah, you're too nice for your own good?" asked Brandy, as Sarah walked towards the elevator.

"Yes, people do say I'm too nice. But I can't be any different than I am," Sarah answered turning back to Brandy. Sarah then entered the elevator waving goodbye to Brandy.

The elevator reached the third floor and Sarah glanced at her watch, she realized she wasn't late at all; it was only 2:55 p.m. She was early, how amazing. She stepped off the elevator to find a room full of women of varying ages, shapes, sizes and colours. Sarah couldn't help but noticing the other women appeared all extremely attractive.

Oh, so I'm not the only one up for the job, Sarah thought as she entered into room. If she had it her way when she left today, she'd have the job despite all these beauties. No second interviews, or third interview. This wasn't a beauty contest after all. She would win this job. She was as sure of it as she was that her name was Sarah Dexler; Sarah thought proudly as she remembered the family Dexler motto, "Venimus, Vidimus, Vicimus". It meant "We came. We saw. We conquered!

Sure, her ancestors had blatantly borrowed the saying from Caesar, but it was a good motto to live by and inspired confidence. Of course, if you could use your God-given charm and win the day why shouldn't you? She didn't think you had to use your attitude violently, or cruelly, like a sword. A charming disposition worked as well, or better than the sword and without drawing blood.

Sarah steeled herself marched up to the receptionist and confidently said… "Sarah Dexler, I have an appointment at 3 p.m."

"Yes, Miss Dexler, your name is here. Please, take a seat. Mr. Poundstone will be with you momentarily," the receptionist said hardly looking up from her desk.

The office door opened and a congenial looking man came out. If Sarah were to describe him, she would describe a dignified Santa, maybe an Edmund Gwenn style from Miracle on 34th Street. His appearance was stylish and dignified, like an upper crust Englishman, suiting his voice on the phone. His suit was a gray Burbury throughout. His hair trimmed short and he had a tiny white moustache. He seemed to be in his sixties.

"Miss Dexler, I presume?" Mr. Poundstone looked straight into her eyes.

"Yes, I am Sarah Dexler," Sarah stood tall and threw her shoulders back, holding out her right hand which he clasped firmly with both his hands.

"I am Harry Poundstone. What a great pleasure to meet you in person. I worried I had steered you wrong, as I remembered not giving you my office number. But I can see you are as good as your word and you obviously found me. Please do come into my office, so, we can discuss the particulars of this job and your qualifications for the position," said Mr. Poundstone, while still smiling.

"Certainly, I would be happy to Mr. Poundstone," replied Sarah while stepping into his office.

Mr. Poundstone continued to smile even more broadly, almost unnerving Sarah.

"Miss Dexler, I didn't want to tell you in front of all those job applicants, but we decided to give the job to you," Mr. Poundstone declared with great flourish.

"Me? But you didn't even interview me? Are you sure?" Sarah was shocked but rambled on, "Well, of course, if you are sure, or you wouldn't have said so. Oh, I'm doing it again. There's just something about you that makes me do that. Oh, did I just say that aloud. Sorry," Sarah, blurted, and then blanching, asked… "Do you still want me for this job?"

Mr. Poundstone couldn't help but be amused.

"Miss Dexler. Or may I call you Sarah?" asked Mr. Poundstone.

"Please do, Mr. Poundstone," Sarah replied

"Please, would you care for some of this freshly steeped tea? Or, would you prefer coffee?"

"Yes, I would love some tea, two sugars and a little cream please," answered Sarah

"Huh, exactly how I made your tea. Most people prefer milk rather than cream. It's Harry actually. Please call me Harry. Mr. Poundstone is so formal," expressed Mr. Poundstone, and then followed quickly with, "Where do you see yourself in five years Sarah?"

"I could lie, and say I see myself in an executive position ;but the truth is I want it all. I want a career that fulfills me and I want children and a husband."

What a weird start to the interview, Sarah thought. Why, oh why, had she mentioned

she desired a husband and children? Was
she sharing things that were too personal?
Were there bounds that were being
overstepped? There had to be something in
the tea, a truth serum perhaps? What was it
about this man? What caused her to blurt out
exactly what she was thinking? What
possessed her? He would think she didn't
want this job and would leave at the first
opportunity.

Sarah continued thinking knowing she
needed to reassure Mr. Poundstone her
priority was this job. "Oh, but I can tell you
I see this position as a real opportunity to
gain experience…"

Sarah wanted to continue, but could not. She
could not hide her suspicion and was
suddenly compelled to ask "Did you put
something in my tea to make me tell you
only the truth and in fact ,say everything
which I am thinking?"

"No, but I'm finding this conversation
absolutely amazing," Mr. Poundstone
replied smiling and Sarah ,suddenly found
his constant smile, slightly creepy.

"What's amazing?" asked Sarah bravely,
"That for some unknown reason, I believe

that you have the power to mesmerize and draw words from people?"

Mr. Poundstone just grinned even wider like he knew a secret, a secret that Sarah didn't know but needed to uncover.

"Holy cow, I can't believe it. That's it isn't it? You have some unusual power and I can feel it. You can get people to tell you what they are really thinking," Sarah exclaimed while truly surprised by her own words.

Mr. Poundstone reached into his jacket and pulled out a pocket watch which he proceeded to open. The watch was gold and attached to a long chain.

"This is truly amazing. I have never encountered anyone with such acuity. Two minutes, that's all it took for you to perceive the unusualness of our conversation. Most people who have any ability require days to detect my power, but you became aware it within less than two minutes."

Mr. Poundstone's next words shook Sarah to her core.

"He said you would be the one. I heard glimmers of your abilities in our phone conversation, but he was absolutely right.

This is so truly, truly astonishing." His voice became high pitched with excitement, almost maniacal, and belied the dignified image he had shown earlier.

"Uh…Ok… I'm going to leave now." Sarah had become slightly frightened of the nature of Mr. Poundstone's behaviour, "But no harm, no foul."

"Oh, please my dear lady, do not be frightened of me or my employer. I know I am not explaining this well but we've looked so long for one like you…"

Sarah found this last statement even more disturbing.

"That's okay but I think I'm going," Sarah replied reaching for the door handle.

"Please Sarah, I beg of you, give myself and my employer another chance. Wouldn't you like to find out the real reason why we chose you? Don't you want to be aware of the untapped power that you alone hold?" Mr. Poundstone begged again with his voice once again deep and compelling.

"No! If you have some deep dark plan for me, you can just forget it," Sarah turned the doorknob and continued to try to make her escape. "Quit trying to compel me. I know you're doing it. I don't understand how you're doing it but I can grasp you are doing it."

"I apologize; but it is sometimes hard to turn off one's gift," Mr. Poundstone stated calmly. "Did you ever wonder where you came from? Who your parents were? Who were your other relatives? Sarah, we know you started life in Foster Care."

Sarah retorted, her fear changing to anger, "How dare you? That…has nothing to do with a job interview. How did you access those records? You didn't even have my social security number?"

"I know a lot about you Sarah Marie Dexler. For instance, I know your real last name is Maidenstone. The Dexler's adopted you when you were four years old, and isn't the truth, before they adopted you, you did not speak."

Tears formed in Sarah's eyes and her anger grew. "I'm going to report you and your agency to the Better Business Bureau, the police, and a lawyer; in that order. You have absolutely no right to snoop into my life."

"I've hurt you and that was not my intention. I know your grandfather and if he could have found you, believe me, he would have. He would have taken you from that foster home. It really wasn't his fault. Your parents disappeared without a trace in America. They were British citizens, born in Coventry, England. Your grandfather was not even aware of your existence. He found out six years after they had perished, that his beloved daughter and her husband had died. He went crazy with grief, and we despaired that we would never get him back again. But he did recover over time, albeit never to the same contented state. But he discovered by searching through numerous records, that she had a given birth to daughter; that daughter was you. And he asked me to find you."

"So, this was all a ruse? There is no job? Of course, there is no job! Why…why am I still here? Did you hypnotize me? All this because you say my so-called grandfather wants to meet me?"

Sarah was going to tell Mr. Poundstone, he was a very bad man, but he cut her off.

"Needless to say, your grandfather waits anxiously to meet you in person. Moreover, he is well aware of your current predicament and has an exciting job…mmm…opportunity, he wants to discuss with you. But I'm afraid, I have been forbidden to share the particulars with you at this time."

"I don't know about this. None of this seems right. A strange man tells me, I possess a grandfather, a grandfather who didn't come forward to me, when I was young? And now he wants to meet me? And then he expects me to just take a job from him?" Sarah composed herself. "I just don't know. This is a lot to take in."

"Think about meeting him. Please," begged Mr. Poundstone. "You won't be sorry if you agree to this meeting. Your grandfather is a wonderful and wise man."

Mr. Poundstone couldn't help but smile slightly at the corners of his mouth but he kept his eyes penetratingly fixed on Sarah's own deep gaze.

Mr. Poundstone mused out loud, "What if I go tell the other applicants to come back another day for an interview for the actual job, I brought them here for?"

"Please don't keep them waiting. If there's an honest job for them at least interview them. I can wait in the lobby," Sarah replied, relieved the other women were not being duped. And, she realized, she was not surprised Mr. Poundstone sensed her concern for those who unwittingly helped him in his duplicity.

"No, please, I have another office here, I'll interview them there. Just please… take your time. Have a cup from the freshly steeped pot of tea and I hope you'll make the decision you will see your grandfather," begged Mr. Poundstone while leaving the room.

"Fine… I'll wait…but I'm still not sure," Sarah exclaimed with exasperation to Mr. Poundstone's departing back.

In a room next to the one where Sarah waited, a man watched through a two-way mirror. From his side he could see her seated in the chair in front of Mr. Poundstone's desk. The man was mature; his hair greyed at the temples and sides, but with a shock of black hair that ran through the middle of his thick mane. He was tall and stood over six feet, possibly as tall as six feet, six inches. He was broad shouldered and lean ,looking while surprisingly well muscled.

He looked to be about sixty, or maybe sixty-five years of age, but he moved with the ease of a much younger man; as he paced back and forth with his focus on the mirror. Dressed in a suit tailored perfectly for him, he exuded confidence. He seemed mesmerized as he intently surveyed Sarah though the glass. He appeared somewhat amused, that he knew Sarah was unaware that she was being watched.

The door opened to the chamber, where the tall man stood watching. Mr. Poundstone walked into this room with a much different demeanour, than the one he displayed when he had earlier greeted Sarah. Mr. Poundstone lowered his head and seemed hesitant to approach. He moved forward cautiously as if any misstep could trigger an explosion like bomb in a minefield.

"This is the one? This is she? No mistakes this time?" the man demanded harshly while taking a seat.

"Yes, my lord, this is the one. I promise there has been no mistake this time. As promised, I supervised this one myself," replied Harry Poundstone, his voice very subservient.

"Good. What did you tell her?" asked the tall man.

"I told her you were her grandfather and you kept looking for her, just as we rehearsed. I told her you grieved for her mother and searched for her as soon as you knew she existed."

"Marvellous Harry, a falsehood that is so close to the truth is always so much more believable," said the tall man pleased.

"I hope this makes up for the failure of my operatives last year?" asked Mr. Poundstone meekly, obviously seeking approval.

"It does if this is truly her!" replied the tall man, Sarah's grandfather. "Does she show any essence of her mother? Or is she only tainted by him?"

"The taint is there my lord. I am sorry my lord…but if there is any of you in her I see none of it." Mr. Poundstone cowered as he said this, expecting to be castigated. He was all too familiar with the consequences of failing to please his master, through words or deeds.

"I'm sure you are mistaken. She is of my line after all. I think I have seen glimmers of myself. If not, while then it is decided," pronounced the tall man, dismissing the matter.

"Must we, Lord Eccklestone?" Mr. Poundstone dared to ask.

"Are you questioning me? You dare to question me?" demanded Lord Eccklestone.

The tall man's face turned purple and his rage consumed the entire room. To Mr. Poundstone it seemed as if darkness surrounded him, only broken by the fierce glower of his lord's penetrating eyes.

"No sir, of course I am not questioning you. I would never dare," replied Mr. Poundstone submissively, mollifying him.

The pair continued to observe Sarah unbeknownst as she waited anxiously in the adjoining office. Sarah found herself consumed by many thoughts that raged incessantly through her mind. A grandfather searched for her? She had family, but a family that took this long to come forward? Could the story really be true, that he just couldn't find her until now? What an incredible story, much like a fairy tale. Those usually didn't end well.

What of Mr. Poundstone? He was to say, a very unusual man. True. Still there was something not quite right about him. At times she felt he seemed a jovial Santa Claus, but could it just be a false persona? If Mr. Poundstone wasn't who he pretended to be, then how could she trust that this man would put her in touch with her real grandfather?

Maybe she should just leave. But if he did know her grandfather and he could put them in touch maybe she should give him a chance? Mr. Poundstone was distinctly odd, almost chilling with this strange power he had. He actually eluded she might have one as well, a power. That, of course, was ludicrous stuff and definitely nonsense. Then there was the fact that he had snooped in her personal business.

He had found out facts that she had never told anyone. It was like stripping her bare. She wasn't happy about that. What did she really know about these people? Only what he, Mr. Poundstone, had told her? She had already found out he had a power that made people believe and do what he wanted them to do; so why was she sitting here waiting for Mr. Poundstone? Or waiting for this man that claimed to be her grandfather?

How trustworthy was a man who manipulated people with some spellbinding ability and made them do what he wanted? She suddenly became afraid again. There was something definitely, not quite right about this, and she felt it down to her very bones. If her grandfather had truly wanted to meet her there was no need for this deception. And why were so many people interested in a companion job? And why were they all attractive young women? These thoughts had just entered her mind. What had prevented these thoughts before? There were just too many things that didn't add up here.

So, what was wrong with her that she hadn't bolted all ready? Mr. Poundstone had used some of his power on her; that was the only explanation. The power that she was starting to believe he really possessed. Was it some kind of hypnotism? She was leaving now, this very minute, before something bad happened.

Just then the door opened to Mr. Poundstone's office and Sarah watched a man enter. He was tall, dark haired, and mysterious looking. His hair was raven coloured, his eyes blue, and piercing, and his gaze centered on her. He was muscular and dynamic looking. He just seemed to be one of those people that drew upon all eyes upon them. Simply put, this man radiated power and one could not help but put all focus on his presence.

It was odd though ,when he came in the room it was like time stopped. She looked at the clock on Mr. Poundstone's desk and realized that it wasn't as if time had stopped, it actually had. The circumstances were getting more bizarre for Sarah the more she went along today. Had she really gotten up this morning, or was this all a dream?

As she gazed upon the man, he spoke…, "Come on then, we have to leave now," he requested of her.

"We…we have to leave now? I don't think so. I have had enough with your weird people. I don't understand what is going on

but I'm not going anywhere with you,"
Sarah reacted, annoyed.

"I don't have time to explain this to you.
You deserve explanations, but we definitely
don't have time. This only lasts so long. It
takes so much power and energy, that it's
very draining. We have to go now. We have
to be away from here before I lose my
power, which could be at any moment," said
the man urgently.

"Again, with the power? I'm getting out of
here but not with you. I don't want to see
any of you weirdoes ever again," replied a
disgusted Sarah.

"Fine, just come with me now. Let us leave
and get away now!" pleaded the man.

"I don't even know your name. I'm not
going anywhere with you. I'm going home,"
Sarah's anger grew and she was very
determined to get away.

"They know where you live. They want
something from that you don't even know
you have," The man then said cryptically,
"They are not nice people. You don't
understand the lengths they will go to or the
things they have done."

"Enlighten me then," Sarah demanded.

"I told you there isn't time. Please I beg of you, come with me now."

"And you are? And I should come with you because? I'm tired of this. You and all these other people just come into my life making impossible demands."

"You can do things that aren't possible or real. Oh…just go away and leave me be"

"My name is Demetrious Blackstone and we are sort of related. I promise I'll tell you more once we are away from here." Then seeing her face, he added, "I know all of this is difficult for you to understand and I will explain when we get away from here but we must get away now."

He then took Sarah's hands and pulled her to her feet. Moments later they are out the door. Sarah wasn't sure how they got to the waiting room so fast. Or even why she didn't fight back and resist but here they were. In this room Sarah saw all the people she had before, but there was still not a ripple of movement.

Time was stood still and it seemed as if only they moved through it. It was all so unreal and peculiar. Demetrious opened the front door of the building and they passed out into the street. Cars were stilled, not moving at all as time and space stood still. Not even a breeze blowing. Sarah was amazed and frightened all at once. What was going on?

"How long will this last?" asked Sarah.

"Not much longer. We must be long away when it stops. He will know it was I and come after us," warned Demetrious ominously.

"I'm going home," insisted Sarah, afraid but determined.

"Do you not understand their fierce abilities? Don't you understand the danger you are in?" Demetrious asked, staring at Sarah.

Then slowly searching her face he sighed and said… "No, of course you don't. How could you know that there is a great peril to you here? This man, who is your grandfather, is kin to a vampire. He finds power from innocents, from those who are not aware of their power. He then takes their power from them and not in a pleasant way,

I assure you. What he leaves of these people is a nothing but a zombie-like creature; a creature that only exists to obey their lord and master; your grandfather. Or, if he chooses, they are left a broken soul whose mind is completely stripped, so they function only on a basic primitive level."

Sarah did not believe her ears and denied everything the man was saying.

"This is all so utterly ridiculous. I'm starting to think that Mr. Poundstone drugged me, so I'm very glad you got me out of there Mr. Blackstone. I thank you for everything you have done so far but I'm going home. Now!"

"I am sorry I have to do this to you. I wouldn't if it wasn't necessary to protect you. But you don't even realize the great power you hold and how and what could happen ,if someone as unscrupulous as your grandfather got a hold of that power."

Demetrious gripped the back of her neck gently with the fullness of his hand and Sarah began to feel light headed. Slowly the world seemed to fade away and she fell into a deep unconsciousness. ~0~

Excerpt from Stray Bullet

The Sheriff Bullet Mystery that began all the books.

In the small town of Driftwood, Colorado, under starry skies, residents went about their business. The town was now ready for the arrival of the new sheriff having gussied up the urban decay with a few coats of paint. The new sheriff would see the bad parts of town soon enough the mayor thought and turned over in his bed and went to sleep. The hospital looking after a few patients was unusually quiet under the full moon; other people in the settlement getting ready for bed and then turning on late night programs or setting alarms and climbing into bed. Across town a man getting ready for bed after a long hard day at work completed his paperwork, stripped naked and stepped into the shower.

As the water ran down in torrents the shower glass doors shattered, the man fell to the floor and rivets of blood ran into the drain. He was the first to die that night.

A few doors over gunman entered killing the husband and wife in their beds and the children as they slept. Blood covered the floor and ceilings in those rooms. None of the neighbours heard a peep they simply slumbered on. Other homes across the town were entered and the residents, husband wife and children were also shot and killed. No one had time to shout out or call 911. It was all over in a few minutes with no time for whimpers only the muzzle of silencers doing their jobs and hitman scurrying into the night.

"It's done, boss. The teams are leaving the state. Yes, I'll do that now. He's coming in the morning. I'll check in after I meet him. His name? All I got is G. Bullet not sure of his first name, it's not on any paperwork. . See you, tomorrow… okay Friday," the man said into his prepaid cell phone and then took out sim card breaking it into pieces. Then he discarded it in a nearby bin at the now decrepit old pulp and paper mill. He had to go to work soon. A new sheriff was coming to town and he wanted to be there to greet him.

~0~

Chapter 1 – Friendship Trumps Bullet

Μy name is G ,and I'm on my way to

a new life to become a sheriff in a town called Driftwood. Sounds boring, doesn't it. If you'd asked me five years ago, I would have told you of course it was; but now this is what I need and my daughter needs…a nice quiet life, in a quiet town, where I could raise my daughter without whispers and rumors. You want to more about that statement? I'll get back to that, but I'm told people will want to know about me a subject I'm not really comfortable talking about.

Asked to describe myself I would say I'm tall over six feet…okay six feet five inches. I am muscular as I lift weights. I'm not overly muscular just enough to take down the bad guys. Some people think I look like

Tom Selleck in his youth, personally I don't see the resemblance.

G. is a short form for my first name but I don't like to talk about my real first name. Let's just say my parents grew up in the happy-go-lucky seventies and were heavily influenced by the weird names that people gave their children. What you still won't give up? You demand that I tell you my first name? You want to play the guessing game?

My first name is unmentionable I don't talk about it ever!! My last name is wait for it...Bullet...I know a clichéd name if you ever heard one. Honestly, it's my name. It has been mine, my whole life.

My last name had raised a few eyebrows can you imagine how many chuckles I've gotten when I tell anyone my full name? Still can't guess? Some of you have deducted correctly. So now you know why I usually don't divulge my first name.

In order for you to understand the relevance
of my last name I'll have to explain more
about my family and their origins.

My grandfather when escaping persecution
in Russia came through at Ellis Island and
decided to Anglicizing his name to Bullet;
so my dad used that and now I do. What's
that you like to know grandpa's original
name? Well so would I, unfortunately he
took that name to his grave leaving no clues
behind. But he was great man, a hard-
working cop. I come from a long line of
cops. With a last name like Bullet it tends to
earn respect, being a cop.

Grandpa was killed on the job by some
backward gangsters bent on destroying one
another. My dad swore he never be a cop
and went to San Francisco were he promptly
fell in love with my mother went to the
police academy there and then impregnated
my mother.

After I turned one ,he decided he needed
family and got a job as a cop in the city

where his father had served and brothers now served as cops. When he worked there for six months he had planned to send for mom and then marry her.

Unfortunately ,the first day on the job, he ran into a domestic situation and was killed in the line of duty. He hadn't told his family, about my mother ,or me ,so we came as a surprise ,when mother showed up with me in tow for the funeral.

When I was four years old, my mother learned she was dying of breast cancer. My dad's three brothers, James, Bennie, and Alfred also cops, stepped up to raise me. They were a demanding bunch always pushing me to be strong and tough. I had to be resilient and learn all the fighting techniques that they taught. Let's say I am proficient in a number of fighting techniques.

Their younger sister, my Aunt Louisa was a teacher and just starting her career when they took me in however Aunt Louise found time for me. She made my childhood more normal though my uncles would often say she shouldn't coddle me. My uncles drove her away with their constant beratement and by the time I was in my teens she moved to teach in Colorado to save her sanity.

She still managed to chide the uncles into letting me visit her in Denver in the summer for two months; the best two months of the year for me.

Getting back to my uncles, they hated my first name, as much as I did (though I think they liked me even less; but did their duty). They also felt that I had come out of nowhere so they nicknamed me Stray and it stuck; that's what most of the cops on the force called me. Aunt Louise was the only one who ever called me; by my first name.

Aunt Louise had recently retired to a small town called Driftwood Colorado and I wished she had been closer especially when I had run into the wall of blue at my job. Cut to today as I told you earlier ,I'd taken a new job as the sheriff in Driftwood Colorado.

As I drove to the Sheriff station; I saw that the downtown area was newly painted but other parts were decrepit and rundown. Stores had been closed and signs had been posted that said for rent but the places looked like they hadn't been rented in a long time. The back alleys showed signs, of hookers working their wares with discarded condoms.

The town was surrounded by trees; but the main source of jobs in the past had been lumber and the company had pulled up stakes and moved away. Factories and brickyards were closed. Some of the homes have seen better days and the downtown core was eerily quiet, with vacant storefronts lining the streets. Crime which in the past hadn't been a problem was suddenly up and maybe that's why the Sheriff had quit? But that was the reason I was here. I'd shape this town into a town we could all be proud of again if the re-elected mayor could do as he promised and bring in the jobs. I wanted to be happy here.

I'd just dropped off my three-year-old daughter with my Aunt Louise. Stella Marie, my daughter seemed okay with the new place and Aunt Louise; but was I? Aunt Louise was sixty years old, and a retired school teacher. Why was I so worried? First day jitters ,obviously. Aunt Louise had my back.

She knew what idiots her brothers really
were and how they valued their friendships
even more than family. Being a single
father, I needed her more than ever.

Aunt Louise had urged me to apply for the
vacant job of Sheriff after hearing about my
troubles as a cop in a suburb of Halton,
Illinois. I don't want to get into those
troubles right now. Today was a new day
and I decided it was going to be great even if
it killed me. Just kidding! I was not going to
get killed like my dad had on the first day of
the job. Nerves were getting to me.

Sure ,it was hard settling into a new place
for a child. A little voice worried that I had
made a mistake; but this was a new start for
both of us we should be happy. A month
ago, I had been offered my dream job,
Sheriff of a small municipality in Driftwood,
Colorado. Driftwood looked to me like a
small town of three hundred people where
I'd be happy raising Stella-Marie.

The streets were tree-lined; the cookie cutter houses had beautiful floral displays out front. The lawns were immaculate green and lush. Children rode their bikes up and down the streets with no fear of predators or gunplay. The people had seemed friendly and warm when I came for my interview for the job. What more could we want? I'd thought.

I'd done my research; but nothing had prepared me for the men all walking out on me. I stepped into the Sheriff's car.

This blue flu wouldn't do! I knew from the dispatcher that the other cops were not happy with my appointment; but damn it was my first day on the job and they had a duty to serve and protect the citizens of Driftwood.

How could the four deputies just not show up for the day? Calls to their residences had gone to voice mail so they were even avoiding talking to me. I had to put my foot down hard or the men would never respect my leadership. I'd already faced a wall of blue in my old job; people pulling out the

old politics line and drawing in ranks on the
thin blue line. I'd wanted a new start to
change the harassment I'd faced in my not
so fair city over the last three years.

A bit of a long story which we'll get into
later but suffice to say the line in blue was
put up against me; simply because I stood up
to another cop who committed a crime.

Driving down the road to go to my new
deputy's home I grew angry. Hadn't I been
through enough of this crap from the guys in
Halton? I had been harassed day and night
by those assholes.

I had to pull myself together, anger would
not solve this problem. I could show them I
was in charge but approachable. I was an
outsider, hired on line. Hell ,I hadn't even
met any of these guys, but I would get along
with them .They just had to give me a
chance.

No ,that sound desperate and I wouldn't be that anxious. I would be the best Sheriff and boss they ever had.

I parked the squad car and mounted the wooden steps on the house. I knocked lightly on Deputy Gregory Barnes door. No answer. I gave it my best thundering police knock and the door swung open of its own accord. I pulled my service revolver and entered the residence wily. A smell of dead berries and apples entered my nostrils. I felt in my pocket and swished my menthol medicated lip balm under my nose. My adrenaline kicked in and suddenly I felt exhilarated and hyper aware.

I followed the putrid odor to a bedroom and found the late Greg Barnes with two bullet wounds to the heart surrounded by a dried rusty brown pool of blood. He'd been there at least two days. Nothing was disturbed in the home. No overturned furniture, nothing seemed out of place. He lived alone; so no help there. Was it a rogue girlfriend? Why was he dead?

What the hell? The first day on the job and my deputy is murdered? I needed those other cops that hadn't come to work today,

to help me solve this murder. Damn them,
and their blue flu!

I made the call to the coroner who was on
call for autopsies. Then I secured the scene
and called in the neighboring counties police
force on loan until I could find my police
force.

Less than an hour later, I had two officers,
Alfred Jones and Paulo Scarlatti, I sent to
the two of them to retrieve the first officer
Joseph Paciocco on my list. Imagine my
surprise when he called back to tell me that
my other officer, Joseph Paciocco was dead
too. Two shots to the heart and it looked like
the same felon. Was I going to find all my
missing officers dead?

A quick search of the other residences found
all of the bachelor cops, dead, shot the same
way. The family men with their families at
home were dead too; but so were all their
family members. They had all been shot
with one shot to the head in their beds. They
had not stood a chance. This was a
professional job, as each scene ,had been
carefully scanned ,and nothing was left to

find in the way of evidence, other than the blood and bullets.

All in all, the dead were Gregory Barnes, Joseph Paciocco, Jack Abrahams, Paul Jones, Harold Jones and his wife Cheryl, their two children Gail, and Fred, Vincent Vecchio and his wife Paula Antrim (both cops on the force), their baby, Adrian a newborn was alive in his crib and was taken into custody of the Children's Aid until a relative could be reached. Also, dead were Robert Di Salvio and his wife Rebecca and their fifteen-year-old son William and their daughter Helen eight years old, Kas Mahmoud his wife Dayita, and their three sons, Aaban, Aahil, and Aatif ages five seven and nine.

What in the hell was going on? Someone had killed whole families. Why? Did they know something someone didn't want them to know? Was it retaliation?

This meant looking into backgrounds and finding out things people didn't want you to know. Being sheriff didn't make for a popularity contest; in any case ,but this would have to be handled very delicately.

The police officers on loan ,couldn't
continue to investigate this. I only had a
temporary loan of their services for today.
Even if I wanted to investigate, I had to have
help. I needed to call the F.B.I .pronto and I
knew just the guy my former partner Gordon
Chum.

I dialed Gordon's number by heart. He
answered on the first ring ,asking me about
the new job and then said he'd speak to his
boss and get the okay to bring a team down,
as soon as possible.

Meanwhile ,I was trying to comfort the staff
left at station, and ducking calls from
reporters from all over the country, and
residents of Driftwood who were demanding
to know what had happened. I took deep
soothing breaths…Gordon would be here
soon we'd get to the bottom of this. Penny
Ambercrombie the office dogsbody and
police dispatcher took charge and hustled
the troops off to their stations ,to work on
the tasks I'd given them.

Penny was tall and lean possibly one hundred and ten pounds though it was hard to tell for her clothes hung on her in nondescript browns that did nothing to enhance her looks and she was well over five feet eleven. Her hair was a rich chestnut and was wound tightly at the nap of her neck into a bun. Her eyes were her most striking feature that not even her terrible clothes sense could hide as they were a glittering emerald green that showed immense interest and intelligence. She appeared to be in her late twenties though her skin was leathered with the weathering an outdoors enthusiast had.

I could see that Penny was an asset to me and the sheriff's station in my job. But first I needed to call Aunt Louise and Stella- Marie and hope my daughter wouldn't get too upset that daddy would not see her until tomorrow at the earliest.

I picked up the phone and called the number by heart. There was no answer. Where could she be I wondered? My question was answered in the next few seconds by my office door swinging open. There my Aunt Louise stood with Stella Marie. Aunt Louise demanded, "Gunnar is it true? Are they all dead?"

The next thing that happened was three-year-old Stella-Marie jumping in my arms and saying "Daddy, I missed you."

I closed my office door no sense in putting on a show to the remaining troops and I hoped no one had heard my aunt utter my first name. Stella-Marie took the chair nearest me.

"I want an answer Gunnar."

"Not in front of the c.h.i.l.d."

"Ch. i. l.d, child, that's me," my precocious daughter answered.

"Stella-Marie already knows all about this. She turned on the television while I was in the bathroom and she heard about all your deputies and their families being found dead. She insisted I bring her here."

"Then you both know what I know. I'm investigating and I've called in the FBI."

"Daddy, are you safe? In that movie with the Kung Fu guy they tried to kill him and then killed his family," Stella-Marie answered.

"What have you been watching?"

"I remember his name. I love Jean Claude van Damme movies," Stella-Marie stated.

"Me too, pumpkin and we're safe. I haven't been here long enough to be mixed up in whatever is going on here," I reassured.

"You'll find the bad guys?"

"Daddy will find them. That's what daddy used to do before he had you," I answered.

"Be careful," Stella-Marie said with adult wisdom beyond her years.

"Stella-Marie is correct. You need to stay safe."

"I promise both of you, I will stay safe."

"We'll trust you."

"Can we have dinner together, daddy?"

"Of course we can, my apple dumpling.

"I'm not an apple dumpling."

"No, you're my little pumpkin."

"You're silly, daddy."

"What would you like for dinner? Pizza? Chinese food?"

"Pizza. I want pizza!!"Stella-Marie chimed.

I ordered her favourite Hawaiian pizza and we forgot work for a few minutes as we ate. Stella-Marie told me about her day between bites. Stella-Marie sounded happy and adjusting well to living in this new place. She didn't seem too worried about my job anymore. She kissed me goodbye and said, "Get'em, daddy. See you tomorrow, nighty, night."

I breathed a sigh of relief my daughter seemed happy despite all that was happening. I was the new sheriff so the danger to me from who ever committed these murders must be minimal if any, so my family was safe. Still, I told Aunt Louise to keep Stella-Marie indoors and keep the doors locked reporting any suspicious activity to me.

Gordon arrived a few minutes later, "I'm Special Agent Gordon Chum FBI," he said showing his badge then continuing he said, "I'm here to take over this case."

"No. You're not you're here to assist me and the good people of Driftwood."

"I am here to serve the people yes and if that means taking over the investigation in a town that has seen fit to kill all its police officers save one..."

"How dare you? This town is peaceable. There is a perpetrator or perpetrators who have committed a heinous crime but we will get to the bottom of this."

"You should have recused yourself Sheriff."

I heard Penny Ambercrombie gasp and then mutter under her breath, "What a maniacal idiot and a kook to boot."

"No, I shouldn't recuse myself!" I replied to Gordon, "This maybe my first day on the job but I am imminently qualified to investigate this. I hadn't even met these men or their families; but I care very much about what has happened to them. They are police officers and my squad. Every one of them is mine so this crime was done against me and my family. Do you understand?"

"I understand the feeling and I promise not to step on your toes, Sheriff. My men and I are at your disposal in this investigation. You are in charge. Perhaps we could discuss the particulars before my colleagues get here?" Gordon stated.

"Please follow me this way to my office, Special Agent Chum," I answered.

"Call me Gordon," my pal offered.

"People call me Stray," I stated.

Gordon pretended to be shocked and lifted an eyebrow at me. Penny looked at Gordon with disgust but went back to the front desk of the station.

Gordon entered my office and shut the door, loudly. Spotting the pizza he said, "That went well."

"Yes, it did. Did you see the dispatcher, Penny Abercrombie craning her head and her ears to listen to you?"

"I saw her ,when I came into the station. She was frowning at you and giving you dirty looks ,when you weren't looking like she didn't believe you belonged here."

"I noticed those looks all day," I answered.

"That should be the end of that you can thank me now. She is directing those looks to me now and I'll wager she'll spread all over town how you defended the honor of the dead."

"Thanks, Gordon, for the assist; but how will we can we keep up the lie?"

"We begin a new friendship," Gordon said calmly then continued, "I hope you saved me a few slices of that I'm starved and my team is checking into the No-Tell Motel down the street within the hour."

I smiled and nodded handing him a couple of slices. It was good to see my old partner again.

"You are staying with me and Aunt Louise, aren't you?" I asked.

"Lucky for you or is it me they are limited space in this town to stay and of course this allows me to begin a new friendship with you. All my agents have taken up the last rooms in the motel so I'm grateful your aunt will put me up. You did ask her didn't you?"

"Didn't think I had to. Aunt Louise loves you."

Gordon raised another eyebrow.

"Fine, I'll call her now."

I dialed and Aunt Louise answered her cell phone on the first ring. Aunt Louise said of course Gordon was staying here. I told her not to tell anyone we knew her and she agreed after I told her why. Then she said she had to go as she had pulled over to answer the cell phone.

"So ,it's settled?" Gordon asked.

I nodded.

"What a terrible first day on the job for you pal," Gordon commented, "Especially after what happened to you more than three and half years ago."

I thought back to what I had been through the last three and half years and I found myself reliving that chaotic time in my mind.

I'd been about eight years on the job in the city of Halton, Illinois, a cop, just like my dad and grandfather and uncles before me. The city had gone to the gangs. . It was two steps and one step forward. Every time we turned around; another shooting another victim of a drive-by. Just the other day the victim was a seven year old kid innocently riding their bike! Luckily the kid lived; but we actively hunted for the shooter or shooters. I should have took that as an omen seeing as my grandfather and my dad lost their lives in the police service, but I went merrily on my way doing my job not expecting my life to come crumbling all around me.

A routine call to a richer neighborhood for a disturbance started it all. The dispatcher didn't think to tell me it was a domestic disturbance and the man had a gun. I'm always careful in those situations; more careful then the average cop but if you don't know you can't take precautions.

I knocked on the door and announced
myself and shots barreled through the front
door grazing my forehead and tearing my
knee apart. I burst through the door grabbed
the shooter and he shot me again. That
should have got me accolades and medals
right? After all I was shot doing my job, but
no, all of those rightly went to my partner,
Gordon Chum. The third shot resulted in a
thigh wound that almost made me bleed out
on the spot if it wasn't for the quick work of
my partner Gordon Chum securing the
prisoner and belting my thigh. Okay, so I got
a medal or two, but Gordon was the real
hero. See why he was the first man I called
when my force had been gunned down.

Gordon is a second generation Asian
American. A good looking fellow and
kinder than most men, he speaks softly and
carries a big stick. People underestimating
him rather walk away unscathed. Gordon
standing at five foot six weighed roughly
two hundred and ten pounds of pure muscle.
He knew every fight technique I knew and
more. He saved my life a time or two.

Gordon was arguably one of the best partners I've ever had. Gordon saved my life after I was shot on duty and secured the scene until back-up could get there. He also called for an ambulance for me. I was carted off to a hospital where I spent the next three weeks in intensive car being prayed over by my fellow cops, and the rest of the city.

Whatever chits they called in with the big guy upstairs it worked, I survived and I should have been happy about that; but all I could think was I missed my moment I was supposed to die like my dad and my grandfather before me on the job. It wasn't that I was that different when I came out of the coma. Okay, so I had a few scars inside and out. My forehead now sported a scar that I could cover with bangs and temporarily bum leg. The leg didn't seem to want heal in fact at one point they threatened to take off my leg; but good old Gordon helped me fight them on that and the knee healed to the point I could walk on it. But it wasn't good enough for work, at least not then.

Suffering from self-loathing (and yes a little
post-traumatic stress disorder, if I truly
admit it); I began to be curt with everyone
closing myself off from everyone and
everything. My wife, Gina took the brunt of
all of this. I was cruel to her at every turn.
When she came to visit I'd ignore her.

I knew I needed help from the police shrink
but I couldn't accept or admit that I, the
wonder boy actually had a problem. Gordon
begged me to quit loathing myself so much
and making everyone else around me
miserable but I didn't listen. I was content to
wallow in my anger and self-loathing.

Weeks went by and Gina seemed unhappy
despite her forced saccharine with me. She
gave me an ultimatum get help; or she
would leave me. I decided I wanted Gina so
I found a shrink of my own choosing Doctor
Collins for his add in the Yellow Pages.

Doctor Collins turned out to be a woman.
Don't get me wrong she wasn't a fantasy
(that blonde fantasy with legs up to here and

hiding behind glasses); no she was more like your grandmother. Non-descript, her silver hair short and curled tight to her head. Her voice was soft and she always offered me milk and cookies before a session. I kind of felt weird at first like she was family and I'd never been all that chatty with family anyway. I had so much trouble talking at first that I'd just sit there and stare at the walls; but after a few sessions she got me to open up about my childhood and then finally about the shooting. I began to feel better and worked on getting my knee back in shape so I could return to work.

I had a routine and I followed it. Therapy followed by afternoon sessions of psychotherapy. With the drugs Doctor Collins prescribed and all our talks I began to almost feel normal again. Okay, so I'm lying; I still had a few stray thoughts that I was a failure and that I should have died; but I labored hard to overcome them and worked on being nicer to my ball and chain. I even began to buy her flowers. As for my leg it was almost good enough to return to work.

Doctor Collins had scheduled my appointment for two p.m. on a Friday and I had looked forward to getting it over with and going home to surprise Gina. A cop buddy had offered me his family cottage and I planned a trip to the Poconos for the next week. I'd already called Gina's work and got her the next week off. It would be a fantastic surprise for her and a chance for us to just lay back and enjoy our weekend. I could even cook all the meals that I caught from the lake as it was loaded with fish.

I decided to change my appointment and let Gina know that it would now be at noon instead of two p.m... Surely I could charm my shrink into seeing me earlier and if not well then I see her next week after my trip. I arrived at the doctor's office to find a note on the door. It seemed my shrink. Doctor Teresa Collins had died suddenly this morning and they were rescheduling. A number to call followed the announcement.

Died! And all they thought about was their schedule? Devastating and only then realizing how close I had gotten with my shrink I fell to the floor crying and took about a half- an -hour to recover enough just to pull myself together. I told myself over and over everything would be okay but I didn't really believe it.

Enough of this shit!! A little therapy and I turned into a wimp; who cried at the drop of a hat. I was a Bullet and we were strong manly types; made of steel not mush!! People died!! Get over yourself I admonished myself. I had a life... a wife who loved me despite myself. It was time to man up and be the husband she deserved. I just had to get away with Gina. I'd go home and surprise her now.

Stopping at the gas station to fill-up and walking into pay I spotted roses. I picked some up and thought how pleased Gina would be. She deserved this after all I'd put her through the last two months. She'd surprised me two weeks ago, telling me that she was pregnant. I was overjoyed looking forward to our baby coming in six months.

We had a new beginning and I would make
her as happy as Gina had made me.

I thought about the look on her face; her joy
at our baby and decided to book her
favourite restaurant before we left town. We
could then leave at nine p.m. I'd drive all
night and we reach there by morning. It
could be done despite my gimpy leg. Okay
so I lied, I wasn't fully recovered; but soon I
would be. My physical therapist was pleased
and said I might even be able to go back to
work in a month.

I went home opening the front door with my
key and... You know what happened? It was
that other old cliché...husband comes home
and finds his wife naked doing the tango
with another naked man.

I didn't recognize him from the back as he
jumped out the window, naked clothes in
hand. She could tell me who he was in her
own good time. And I had plenty of time as
I seethed and wanted to kill him but not her.
I didn't want to hurt her at all I just wanted

to take her in my arms and make this go away.

I took huge breaths and then realized it takes two to tango. I had brought this on with neglect and coolness towards her when all she did was support and love me. I took deep breaths to calm myself and rationalized. I was sure this was just a one-time thing.

I'd heard women could get quite horny in pregnancy I obviously had let her down.

I had been a terrible husband moody brooding, distant and angry. Gina deserved better and I could forgive her this. Couldn't I? Sure I was angry, but I would never harm Gina despite my thinking for her lapse in judgement. I had stared at her five foot nine naked figure with its well-endowed breasts and tiny waist and wondered how she hid our baby in it.

Her curly black hair fell in ringlets to her waist. I realized I loved her. I loved our baby. It had been my neglect that had driven her to this; I was prepared to forgive her and take her on my planned trip. We'd been married fifteen glorious years, okay so not glorious, fiery but she was also pregnant and I wanted my child to have a stable home with two parents one of them me. I'd been spared so my kid could grow up with a dad it was as simple as that.

I told Gina all of this and she laughed. It seems that she and her paramour had been carrying on since day one of one of our marriage. Once more she had an amniocentesis last week and received the results this morning the baby was his not mine. I was devastated all those dreams of playing catch with my daughter. Taking her to daughter and daddy dances. Having her look up to me, with hero worship came crashing down. Yes, I know it could have been a boy; but I had my heart set on a girl.

I admit it I went against all my principles and begged her to stay and claim the baby was mine. We were married so the baby was legally mine. She laughed that twinkly laugh that I knew so well and I had to restrain myself from retaliating as she told me she already left me I just hadn't noticed. Gina said she was tired of living a lie. Now that I knew it was all out in the open and she file for divorce and move in with him. She lunged at me slapping me and asked why could I be like him?

I want to hit back at her but I couldn't if I it back I wouldn't be any better than the men I arrested who abused their wives.

Why couldn't I be like him? The man that she slept with she raged at me. I was stupefied and getting angrier by the moment I knew I needed to leave before I regretted losing my temper; but I needed to know who had replaced me.

She laughed again and said I find out soon. I begged her to tell me and she did.

HIM? I fell to my knees. How could it be
him? No, it wasn't Gordon Chum; but
someone else I considered a friend and
brother. Gordon wouldn't do that to me. The
dirty dog who had betrayed me had been a
partner, a mentor and good grief the man
was old...fifty-five if he was a day, and close
to retirement.

Why had she cheated on me with my former
partner Derek? He'd broken the cop code
you didn't sleep with another cop's wife.
He'd slept around I heard how many women
he'd been with had she? I told her and she
laughed telling me it was his cover story.
She continued snickering and said at least
every woman didn't try to pick him up in
front of her. She packed her bags and then
trounced out the front door to join him at his
house.

I thought I could handle it all and maybe I
could have if she hadn't come back a half an
hour later saying she'd changed her mind.
She stripped to her skivvies and begged me
to change her mind. What's a hot-blooded
male to do? I wanted to prove I was the

better man, the better lover, so I turned my back and began stripping too.

That's the last thing I remember ,before waking up in hospital. How I got there and what happened after that I couldn't recall until much later.

The doctor kept speaking to me, but it sounded like gibberish. My brain didn't want to understand. I don't know why. I closed my eyes, but before I drift under, I hear them talking.

"Will he be okay now, doctor?" Gina asked.

"We'll know better when he answers my questions," I perceived the doctor say, far away.

I heard footsteps as someone left.

A voice I recognize as Gina whispered in my ear, "You stupid son of a bitch. Why didn't you die? You'll wish you had now."

I struggle to wake before she can harm me but it's like moving under quicksand. I hear

an alarm sound and footsteps run into the
room.

"What did you do you now, you evil bitch?"
I heard Gordon yell as I feel myself falling
through layers of unconsciousness into
nothingness.

~0~

Excerpt from Dreams Can Kill
Chapter 1- Survival

T he rain pelted down on me, as I

struggled to come to my senses. My head felt like it had split in two, as if little lumberjacks had taken up residence. I opened one eye. The world spun sideways like a ride at the fair. I tried shutting one eye, then the other. I nearly fell back to sleep. I opened my eyes again, fighting the sleep which wanted to overtake me. I shuttered my eyes again, as my stomach protested. My whole body manipulated, bruised, bent and broken like some old rag doll discarded.

Sleep...sleep would solve my problems, my brain protested. No! I had a reason I needed

to stay awake and alert...A little sleep, a part
of me protested again. No, I must stay
conscious. But I remained so tired. I dragged
myself across the pebbled ground. My right
leg stuck out at an impossible angle,
obviously broken. I saw by lifting my head
slightly and turning it that there appeared to
be a road up ahead. I had to get to the road.
If I dragged myself that far, surely, I would
be rescued?

But it was oh so hard, to drag yourself
backwards, when you couldn't perceive
where you were going. Oh no, what if he
came back. He would finish me off...finish
what he had started.

He who? Who was this person, who left me
to die? Why couldn't I remember? Don't
panic… the thing to do is right now is to
reach help; then and only then would I be
safe.

I caressed large pieces of gravel which cut
into the back of my head. I sensed I was
close to the road. I reached out with my
good hand and touched a paved surface.

I knew I didn't have much strength left. I experienced the energy drain quickly leaving my body. I tried to fight the drain, but the world faded to black.

~0~

Chapter 2- Time Flies When You're Having Fun

I opened my eyes slowly A tube

appeared to have been inserted in my arm, feeding me intravenously, another tube down my throat as well. The lumberjacks in my head had been replaced by a dull achy sensation, as if I wasn't quite there. I suffered from weakness all over, but my body didn't have the same sensation, as when I had blacked out on the road. My leg felt whole again and yet my leg didn't appear to be in a cast, or slung up on a tripod. How much time had passed? This definitely looked like a hospital room. The walls were pale white and I lay in a single bed. I rested in a private room how about that?

A nurse in a white cap entered the room. She grabbed my wrist and she proceeded to take my pulse. Alarmed, she stared straight into my face, "Well! Look who is awake. Welcome back to the real world," she proclaimed.

I tried to speak and realized the tube in my throat prevented that. Why was a tube in my throat I wondered? How long I been here? I assumed I looked scared because the nurse explained in a soft voice, "There, there honey, you take deep breaths, easy now."

"Why don't I go get the doctor? He can come and have a look at you and remove the tube from your throat."

I tried to nod my head in agreement but my head moved like lead. It seemed like eons before a man in a white doctor's coat appeared at my bedside. He appeared tall and lanky; with dark curly brown hair and warm deep blue eyes. Without any preamble he announced, "We will now remove this tube. Take a big breath now."

The tube came out as I gagged. Now I could ask the questions which plagued me.

"How did I get here? And, where am I?" I tried to ask, croaking out the words, as if my voice hadn't been used in a while.

"Speak slowly. Here, have sips of water," answered the doctor.

"How did I get here?" I repeated, sure that I had been speaking clearer because I had taken a sip of water.

"I don't know who found you, but an ambulance brought you here in critical condition. You had a broken leg, some broken ribs, and a fractured skull."

"I came here in critical condition? So, I've been here awhile?" I asked shocked.

"Yes, you've been here awhile. You were at a different hospital first. You are in Andrews' clinic now."

"Your condition appeared to be perilous there for some time. They lost you twice. We had placed you in a coma to let your brain swelling go away. Then we didn't know if you would ever come out of the coma."

He continued to explain like he couldn't quite find the words. But why would a doctor have trouble explaining a medical condition?

"I guess time flies when you have fun," I stated flippantly, hiding fear I didn't quite understand and becoming puzzled.

Why did he say first they then we? Hadn't he been there?

"I would like to examine you to see how you're doing now and get an update on your condition."

"I'm good. As you can see," I answered in response.

"I don't know if you even realize, but your speech isn't as clear as you think. You're slurring your words," he stated, "I'm sure the words will come easier in time, but I'd like to check your reaction time and some other physical reactions."

What could he be talking about? I wasn't slurring my words. Was I?

The doctor began his examination. A flashlight flashed deep into my eyes. I blinked in response, as the light, so bright, made my eyes hurt. His response seemed to be to write down something on the chart, and pick up my wrist to take my pulse and blood pressure. He then listened to my chest with his stethoscope.

I moved my head and tried to sit up, but the effort zapped all my remaining strength. I surprised myself at how I felt like a newborn baby. He continued his examination. I grew tired but fought the sensation. If I closed my eyes for a moment, would the feeling would go away? I closed my eyelids and fell fast asleep.

I ran over hills. The night appeared so dark, and ink black; I could barely view two feet in front of me. My feet stumbled, as I tried to see the uneven ground in front of me. My palms clenched with sweat, as my heart pounded like the organ would jump out of my chest. I turned around, my eyes darting from side to side searching for my pursuer. No sign, but I knew he wasn't far behind.

My hair in a high ponytail, whipped at my
face, as I picked up the pace in my flight. He
seemed close enough, that I had the
sensation of his breath on my neck… so
close he might reach out and touch me. I
turned again to see if I could glimpse him
near, and I saw a man. But what puzzled me
was what materialized in the man's face.
Where his face should be, a gaping black
hole yawned.

 How could this be? The thought plagued me
only for moment, as fear gripped me and
survival instinct kicked in. Realizing if he
caught me, I would be killed, I ran
stumbling over rock and uneven ground.
When the inevitable happened, I tripped
falling to my knees. He had me. There was
no escape from my fate. I would die now. I
struggled as he grabbed my left wrist
twisting my arm.

This appeared no dream, I might awake
from; he had me now and he would kill me.
I twisted slightly trying to free my wrist but
he grabbed my other wrist and shook me
slightly saying…, "Quite a dream you were
having, but a dream none the less. Nothing
can harm you now."

I stared into his face and slowly his look changed, from the faceless man, to another face entirely. This wasn't the man in my visions; the demon in my nightmare. I knew in my heart this remained an altogether different kind of man.

This face with smiling blue eyes radiated warmth, and kindness. His face stayed gentle, not violent. I had been dreaming and had mistaken his touch for the man in my dreams. I flushed with embarrassment.

"You are quite awake now? I won't harm you. Now, do remember me?"

I stared at him, slowly waking up, and realizing where I was.

"I'm your Doctor, Doctor Andrews, at your service, my lady. We met before when you awoke from your coma," he continued speaking softly, and gently, bowing at the waist and smiling.

Shouldn't I have recognized him immediately? Heat rushed to my cheeks, as I turned red in embarrassment.

I was a fish out of water. I didn't like the
way I reacted; like something had happened
and all was a secret to me. I liked to be in
charge of my life every aspect, and right
now it seemed like I appeared in charge of
nothing.

"How long have I been here?" I whispered,
trying to speak louder.

"I would have said it's a lot longer, than you
think," he replied cryptically.

"Do you always answer a question with a
question? I want an answer for my query," I
demanded angrily.

"What do you remember?"

"I believe I asked you to stop making this an
interrogation. If you must know, I remember
waking up a little while ago the nurse came
in and then you came a little later," I
answered exasperated, wondering what
could be wrong with me. I didn't get angry
so easily. Did I? Why did I behave this way?
Everything he said seemed to make me
angry.

"Your little while ago was two days ago...,"
he explained, breaking off as if afraid to say
more.

"But that's impossible..."

"You fell into a restorative sleep. It is not uncommon for patients who have been in a coma to do so."

"Two days? I slept for two days?" I commented incredulously.

"Yes," Doctor. Andrews stated.

"How long was I in a coma?" I asked worried to hear what he might say.

"What month do you remember?"

"You have to be in charge, don't you? Questions! Questions!" I replied, delaying the answer. I was suddenly afraid that I'd been in this coma far longer than I realized, and grew angrier.

"I know you're scared. Are you sure you want to know? The information can wait," he insisted.

"I'm not scared," I lied with false bravado, "I remember quite clearly the month is March."

"It is the eleventh of September nineteen hundred and seventy-one. Do you remember what happened the day of the accident?" he asked.

"That's not possible. I can't have been in a coma for six months. Why do you lie to me?" I spat at him.

"I know it's hard to assimilate but time has passed and it is September," he insisted softly, but firmly.

"Why do you persist in a lie? What do you have to gain with this preposterous story?" I demanded; still not ready to believe this.

"Exactly what do I have to gain? Sharron, I'm not lying to you," he stated sadly.

Until that moment I hadn't given any thought to my name, but as Doctor Andrews called me Sharron, I realized I wasn't even sure if that was my name. I didn't have a clue what my name was. My name might be Sharron, but I didn't recall the name. My name could be Mary, or Angela, or any other name in the world. If I had a surname, I couldn't remember it either. A huge blank spot stood where any recollection should be.

How could my last memory be of March,
but I still had no recollection of my name, er
names? This was normal after a long coma. I
decided.

Perhaps my memory had been so underused,
and only had temporary gaps? Or I was
hungry? Yes, it had to be one of those
things. A temporary aberration of the mind...
No need for me to worry. No, need to share
any such information.

My memory was only hiatus. That had to be
the answer. Give it a few days and my
memory would all come back. There was no
need to tell the doctor, especially since my
recollections would all come back.
Absolutely not, I reasoned.

After all what good would it do to tell him?
He'd look at me either with sympathy, or
call in a shrink. I wanted none of the
sympathy, and whispered glances which
would follow. So, I had a few memory gaps,
nothing to worry about. It was perfectly
normal after a coma, I reassured myself.

"What will you do with all this information
Sharron?" asked Doctor Andrews suddenly
concerned.

"I must admit the information was a bit of a shock to find the month was September and not March, but I'm over the surprise. "I'm hungry what does it take to get food around here?'' I demanded, quickly changing the subject. Besides I was ravenous.

"I think you can start some light foods, some soft foods, Jell-O soup etc.," Doctor Andrews spouted. Turning to the nurse he commanded, "Nurse get a light meal for my patient."

"Certainly Doctor," the nurse replied, coming into the room rather quickly, at his summons.

Just when I thought I had successfully gotten rid of the doctor, he turned around and said... "I know you are rather tired and hungry right now, but I'm sure you to want to discuss these revelations later today."

How could I get him to change his track? I didn't want to discuss my memory loss with anyone. I wasn't ready for anyone to find out I didn't know who I was. If I told him, would he treat me like a mental patient?

No, I wasn't going to tell him, or anyone. I needed to fake what I remembered. They'd never know, I couldn't remember. I would then have the time to accept this myself, and hopefully everything would come back. No one would ever have to know.

Wait a minute, did he know, I didn't remember? He talked about the fact I'd been in a coma, but had he given me any knowing glances? I gave him a sideways glance. Deciding he didn't have a clue about my memory problem. I plotted to keep it that way.

"There is not a lot to talk about; but if you want to, we can discuss my medical condition we can get to that later," I replied, hoping he would take my response as an agreement and leave.

Luckily for me he took the hint. Maybe he would even forget to come back and discuss this later? No, I hoped for too much, but he did look convinced that I'd talk to him later. Good then he'd go away.

"I will return later, Sharron."

He then left taking his questions with him. I breathed a sigh of relief. Now alone with my thoughts, surely, I'd conjure up a memory or two. First, I would eat and refuel. That would help the memories, as well as my stomach.

I stared at the food the nurse had brought in. I'm starving to death and the nurse gave me not enough food to feed a rabbit? I tried to pick up the spoon and found my hand wouldn't cooperate.

"Would you like some help?" the nurse asked kindly.

"I can do it myself," I responded stubbornly.

Although I had found it difficult to raise my hand to my mouth, that soon became easier. I found by clamping my hand around the spoon I could manage to feed myself. It was then I realized how much work I had ahead of me. The nurse watched, so I smiled at her like everything was fine. She smiled back and left.

I soon made short work of the food and wanted to move on to the therapy I recognized I needed. I would set the memories, or lack of them aside, and working on building up the muscle tone and abilities I'd lost. When the body restored itself, I would begin to remember. I understood without being told, that I had to begin like a baby to exercise my limbs and I wanted to start immediately. Let's be honest. I realized I could remember something. I grasped now that I was an impatient person, at least when it came to doing things I had to be doing. I called the nurse on the call bell to ask about therapy and exercises.

"Yes?" I heard a disembodied voice somewhere over my head say. Momentarily puzzled, I then realized the voice came from an intercom.

"Sorry to bother you but when can I start therapy? I need to get my limbs moving," I explained.

"Dear, you are barely out of coma. I'm sure your doctor would want you to build up your energy first. Or wait at least until you started solid foods."

She sounded surprised and had a hint of censor in her voice. No support there. I wanted those six months back, but clearly that wasn't going to happen. Move on, I told myself. I'd wasted six months sleeping, time to fight back and get back into fighting form as they said. But who had said that?

I somehow knew I was a fighter. I'd have to do everything myself; something I knew I always did. But how did I know that?

I thought about what would work, and what limbs need to work. My hands needed to a work out. Okay, they need to grip. How do you make hands stronger?

You give them something to grip. Squeezing something soft, medium soft, would work. Where to get something to work my grasp? I couldn't even get out of bed. My limbs were useless, absolutely useless.

My hand shook in weakness, from forcing the stupid thing, to do its job and feed me.

All of this began to feel hopeless. No, I wasn't some stupid helpless female. I had to figure out a plan. You're on your own, I told myself, nothing new. You can overcome any odds. Think, Sharron, think!

How about some finger exercises? Slowly working each finger, and then in tandem, I would get back movement. I began the exercise I devised. It sounded so simple when I had thought of how to exercise the hand, but painful and tiring. Work through the pain, I told myself. Isn't that what you've always heard?

I forced myself to do the exercises for what seemed like hours, until I couldn't take the pain any more. Then I decided to exercise my arms. Gripping well enough to pull myself up to the bar over my bed, I reached I'm with my right hand to grab the pole. My fingers won't cooperate. My fingers are weakened and my grip slipped. Damn it! Even simple exercise was impossible.

"Nothing is impossible," a voice spoke loudly in my head. But whose voice did I hear? My memory had fled, if it was ever there. I only comprehended the voice had been someone I loved, and respected. Was this a father, or a father figure? I knew I was bone weary, and a great sea of lethargy stole over me. It would be counterproductive not to take a nap, I reasoned. Surely a short nap would restore my energy and I would begin again.

I closed my eyes soon I began dreaming. At first the dream appeared happy. I viewed myself in a beautiful home and grinning at someone I couldn't see.

I smiled and felt great joy, but the sky grew dark and I found myself outside on a field. The moon overhead slowly covered by clouds, and I grew terrified. Something was wrong. The faceless man chased me once more. I ran over rocks and streams and more rocks. He kept coming and coming. I knew he'd soon be on me. He nearly had me when I willed myself to wake up saying… This is a dream and I want to wake up now.

I awoke gasping for air, like I had been running a marathon. A strange man sat by my bed. His hair appeared dark, practically black, greasy, and slicked back. He had black thick glasses that he peered over like they were a prop.

An oversized suit coat in plaid and matching pants completed the picture. Despite his harmless appearance, he struck terror to my heart. What gave me the idea he put on this persona, like a piece of new clothing? I think it was his face which seemed to give it all away, like he tried too hard to portray someone he wasn't.

As I gazed at him, he jumped from the chair he sat and exclaimed… "About damn time you woke up out of the coma Sharron. I thought you laze there forever."

He then continued, as if choosing his words carefully, "Oh Sharron, this is the most wonderful day of my life." Then he pulled me to him, fiercely.

"Let go of me, this instance. Who do you think you are? I said don't touch me! And quit acting and looking around there's no audience for your play," I blurted out, before I stop myself.

"Sharron, that's not funny. Quit joking. You always had a wicked sense of humour, but I'm not laughing." the man stated, sounding annoyed, and grabbing my wrist.

"I said let me go, and I meant every word. Now kindly take your hands off me," I demanded at the top of my lungs, struggling unsuccessfully to free myself of the grip, he now had on my wrist.

Taken back by my yelling, he let me go, but he still continued to treat me, like a bug under a microscope. Suddenly switching gears, his face changed. It was if a curtain went down over his face. He took on a concerned look and then a hurt look. I admit he nearly had me fooled.

I started thinking I had forgotten a boyfriend, but surely, I wouldn't suffer from such bad taste.

He wasn't my type. He seemed quite violent too. I wouldn't have been so foolish to get mixed up with a weirdo like him! Would I?

"Sharron quit staring at me that way; you're making me uncomfortable. I'm not amused here...Wait a minute ,you're not kidding. You don't recognize me at all. You don't recognize your fiancé?"

I recognized somehow that he was put on an act. No, I wasn't engaged to him. If I had been, it would boggle my mind. He had to be lying, I decided. Why I didn't know, but I knew he lied.

I had no sparks with him. In fact, something about him gave me the creeps. He repulsed me and made my stomach hurt. He certainly didn't sound sincere. He put on an act ... but why? He grabbed my wrists again, once again in a vice grip. I struggled valiantly, but his grip tightened and I couldn't handle his fierce clutch in my weakened stated.

"Let me go you, caveman. I don't know you and what is more, I don't ever want to know you," screamed at him fighting frantically.

"Sharron, you cut me to the quick. Why do you say such things to me?" he whined, letting go of my wrist, but gripping my arms even tighter.

Maybe it was because of my dream, but suddenly I was terrified. Why did they leave me all alone with this crazy man? Where was everyone else? Couldn't they hear me shouting?

"Let me go. Let me go.... Don't touch me," I yelled at the top of my lungs, and then screamed, hysterically "Help me someone help me."

As I started to pull harder frantically to be free, he stilled held fast. What kind of evil demon had me in his grasp? I tried to bite him, but that was impossible; finally, in the answer to my screams were footsteps running. Seconds later a nurse and Doctor Andrews entered.

"Let my patient go immediately. I said let her go," Doctor Andrews growled, pulling the man's arms behind his back.

I breathed a sigh of relief. I was safe. Doctor Andrews had saved me.

"I wasn't hurting her! What kind of a man do you think I am? Gee, I have more bruises than her. She acted crazy, so I grabbed both her arms to calm her," the man explained, sounding plausible.

Surely Doctor Andrews and the nurse who followed him in, didn't believe his act?

"Your technique doesn't seem to have calmed her, but it certainly frightened her," Doctor Andrews said, checking my blood pressure and heart rate.

"You can't tell me what to do. She's my fiancée I can speak to her anyway I want," complained the man, loudly.

"You've upset my patient. Her blood pressure and heart rate are elevated as well. This is not good for my patient, so I can tell you what to do. What is your name?" demanded Doctor Andrews.

"Titus Brown is my name and Sharron is my fiancée," the man replied a little too quickly.

Doctor Andrews consulted his clipboard. He pointed to it and then announced, "This is the approved register and you're not on the list. Leave now, Mr. Brown, or I'll have security escort you out of the facility."

"I'm not going anywhere. Who do you think you are?"

Mr. Brown showed his true colours, I thought. They would trounce him faster than you could say Jack Robinson.

"Mr. Brown, so far, I've been pleasant. The nurse has already called for a security guard. I suggest you leave now and don't come back, or you will find yourself with a trespassing charge and jail time," Doctor Andrews said through his teeth.

"I'll be back with my lawyer and you'll be sorry," Mr. Brown menaced.

Two security guards entered and forcefully removed Mr. Brown from my room. I began to shake like a leaf. I tried to stop, but I grew frightened. Someone had tried to kill me and that is why I was in the hospital. What if it was Him!! Mr. Brown?

They wouldn't let him take me when he talked to his lawyer? Would they? Words I hadn't wanted to share, spilled out of my mouth, first in torments, and then at a screeching level.

"I don't know who the heck he is, but I do know I don't know him. I'm not his fiancée. Don't let him come back lawyer, or no lawyer. I don't want to see him. Someone did this to me! I wouldn't be surprised if the person was him!" I guess I appeared a little too hysterically and forcefully, because the next thing that occurred was Doctor Andrews plunged a needle into me.

"Please, please don't. It's not necessary, really. I'll be good," I pleaded too late.

"It's a little sedative. I don't like your colour, your blood pressure, or your heart rate. You've had a nasty scare and your body isn't able to cope with this right now. Calm down now," he said comforting "Go to sleep."

"I think I hate you," I replied vehemently.

"That's okay, you can hate me if you need to," he answered, smiling.

Damn him and his handsome smile! Something about the grin, made me want to smile back and tell him all my secrets.

"Don't leave me alone. He might come back," I pleaded as I drifted into a deep drugged sleep.

~0~

If you enjoyed Ground Burst, please consider leaving me a few words at your favourite retailer and if you liked the excerpts and would like to read more of my books please check out one of my other books listed on the next page at Amazon at your favourite realtor.

Sincerely S. G. Lee.

~0~

List of Books by S. G. Lee

<u>Murder Mysteries:</u>

The Kelly Murder Mysteries

Book 1-A Penny Saved A Murder Earned

Book 2- A Diller A Dollar A Really Dead Scholar

Book 3- Betty Blue Lost Her Holiday Shoe

Book 4- What Will Poor Robin Do?

Book 5- This Little Piggy Had None

Book 6- This Little Girl Had A Little Curl

Book 7~ London Bridge Is Broken Down

Coming 2026~ Book 8-The Butcher the Baker, the Candlestick Maker

The Kelly Murder Mysteries-Books 1-3

The Kelly Murder Mysteries Books 4-6

A Stitch in Time ~ prequel

The Stone Chronicles

Book 1 -Love's Labour's Won

Book 2- A Tiger's Heart Wrapped in a Player's Hide

Reborn – a novella~ prequel

Stand Alone Mystery/Thriller

Dreams Can Kill

The Sheriff Bullet Series

Book1- Stray Bullet

Book 2- Untraceable

Book 3- Dead Center

Book 4- This Book- Ground Burst

Book 5 - External Ballistics -Coming 2027

Short Story Books

Murder Most Fowl

Jack be Nimble

Day of the Dead

Legends, Folktales and other Stories

The Stuff of Nightmares

ObsessionX2

<u>Christmas Stories</u>

Christmas is Calling

The Christmas Card

The Christmas Angel

Visions of Sugarplums

<u>Poetry</u>

A Poetic Touch - The Human Condition

Poetry in Motion ~ A Forest of Feelings

In the Garden

<u>Children's Books</u>

Mare the Hare

Henrietta and the Donor Egg

The Magical Life of Me

Hello, Baby I'm Your Big Sister

~0~